DARKN

FALLS

DARKNESS FALLS

Heather Schwartz

TATE PUBLISHING
AND **ENTERPRISES**, LLC

Published by Tate Publishing & Enterprises, LLC
127 E. Trade Center Terrace | Mustang, Oklahoma 73064 USA
1.888.361.9473 | www.tatepublishing.com

Tate Publishing is committed to excellence in the publishing industry. The company reflects the philosophy established by the founders, based on Psalm 68:11,
"The Lord gave the word and great was the company of those who published it."

Book design copyright © 2015 by Tate Publishing, LLC. All rights reserved.
Cover design by Lirey Blanco
Interior design by Jomar Ouano

Published in the United States of America

ISBN: 978-1-68187-084-7
Fiction / Action & Adventure
15.10.05

To my mom, Becky, who sadly lost her battle with breast cancer. She was my mom, my best friend, and my biggest fan.

To my mother-in-law who is also a breast cancer survivor, a friend and like a second mom.

To survivors everywhere, your strength amazes me.

PROLOGUE

I t was dark and late. I was so happy Kevin had offered to walk me home. We were almost there, and I wasn't looking forward to saying good-bye. I wanted more time with him; I was trying to slow down enough so that it would take longer but not enough that he would notice.

I'm so silly, I thought, shaking my head; I'm a grown woman. I should just be able to tell him that I like him. I took a deep breath and held it. I reached out and grabbed his arm to stop him and turn him toward me. Even in the dark, I could see his eyes. I took a step away as I sucked in a breath. I should run or scream, but all I could manage to do was stare into those black depthless pits. It all happened in one motion. One second he was standing in front of me, the next he had me in his arms running. I didn't understand. I never saw him move. *How is that possible?*

"Jason will be happy to see you, angel," he said in a voice so gruff I barely heard him. *But who is Jason?*

"Rachel, can you hear me?"

Shaking my head, I tried to pull myself out of the vision. I hated when I was pulled into someone else's mind. It was very disconcerting to hear and feel other people's thoughts and feelings. I could hear her, but I couldn't respond. All I could do was watch as he ran with her. I could see the fear etched on her face, feel her panic, and I already knew her fate. I wanted to run after them, scream out to her. I wanted to save her, but I knew I couldn't. Slowly I opened my eyes. "Rachel, hey, where did you go? Oh my god, you're bleeding."

"Huh?"

I could hear her, but my brain still didn't understand. I was lost in the fog until I licked my lips and tasted the coppery hint of blood I had grown to know all too well. With a shaky hand, I reached up wiping the blood from my nose.

"Rachel, are you okay? Do you want me to get someone?" my best friend, Brooke, asked.

"Um…yeah…no. I'm all right. Just a headache. You know, it's getting pretty late. I should probably be heading home." I wasn't in the mood to explain what was going on. Regardless, I didn't know how to, and I was tired of making up lies.

"Oh yeah, I guess it is getting late. Are you sure you're okay?" Brooke asked, glancing at the clock on the television.

"Yeah, girl, are you kidding me? I'm all right, like I said. Just a little tired," I tried to encourage.

"Do you want to just stay here tonight?" she asked apparently concerned.

"Nah. I'm good. I'll see you later."

After hugs and good-byes, I left the warmth and comfort of my friend's house for the cold, wet dark streets. As I walked home, I thought about what I just saw. I thought about my life and tried to figure out where to go from here. I didn't know the girl in my vision. I had never seen her before in my life, yet she looked so familiar, like from a dream that I can't quite remember. I've tried to keep track of the people I've seen in my visions over the years. Not by names—I very rarely know their names—but by description. I'm not sure why I do this; I just felt that I had to. I felt I had a responsibility to them. I felt like it was my fault they had been taken. I don't know, maybe one day they would all come back, but I didn't have a lot of hope for that, seeing as how I had seen at least half of them tortured to death. Always they were asked the same questions: "Where is she?" "How do we find her?" "Why are you protecting her?"

I had no idea who this *her* was, but I wished they would just tell them what they wanted to know. No one life is worth all of this death and destruction.

Life is dark now, or so they say. I don't think much of it; it's what I've always known. Some say it's the end of days. They say people are disappearing and dying more often than they used to. I try not to think about it; it just seems depressing and sad, so I try to ignore it. I don't need more depressing and sad stuff; my visions had given me enough for ten lifetimes. No one seemed to know what was going on, or at least they weren't telling me. The adults wouldn't talk about it much, and when they do, they appeared quick to change the subject when someone would walk into the room. Sometimes, when I'd walk into a room, I get the distinct impression that they were just talking about me or something that they prefer to keep hidden from me. I had my suspicions that there was something that the people I loved were trying to hide from me. However, I was not sure how to go about finding out what it was or if I wanted to know for that matter. There were more times than I could count that things simply didn't add up.

I knew from a young age that I wasn't the same as my friends, but it was the strange small things that made me different, or at least they used to be little things—things that I knew if I told anyone I would suddenly find myself in a nice padded cell, so I decided to keep them to myself, or at least I tried to.

I can still remember the first time I told my dad of some of the weird things I could do. I was only four at the time, and it hadn't occurred to me not to tell anyone. I couldn't describe the look on my dad's face when I told him; it was something between shock, fear, and admiration. I could understand the shock and fear; I had felt those things myself, but the respect was the one I still don't understand. I mean, what kind of parent would find admiration in their four-year-old telling them that they see people's deaths before they happen. It was after that day that I swore I would never tell another soul if something like that ever happened again, and so far I haven't.

I wanted to tell my best friend once; it was about three years ago when she let me in on her family secret. I can still remember it like it was yesterday. Brooke and I had been hanging out in my room listening to music and talking about boys.

"Hey, Rach, can I tell you something totally weird and crazy and you believe me?" Brooke asked out of the blue.

"Brooke, you're my best friend. Why wouldn't I believe you?" I asked, sitting up and laying down the magazine I had been reading to look at her.

"Because, girl, this stuff is crazy. I'm talking the-cow-jumped-over-the-moon crazy."

"Okay, now I have to know. Tell me, tell me, tell me," I said as I sat up on my knees and leaned toward her, knocking the magazine I had been looking at to the floor.

"Um…okay, so you know the Salem witch trials?" she asked, making me feel a little stupid.

"Of course, Brooke, who doesn't?" I responded.

"Right, okay, so it turns out my great-great-great-great-great-grandmother, or something like that, was one of the first witches burned," she explained.

"Wow, dude, that sucks. I'm sorry, but what's weird about that? I'm sure there are lots of people who can say the same thing. I think it all sucked and was stupid personally.

Did you know most of the people they burned weren't even witches?" I asked her.

"Rachel, focus," Brooke reminded me.

"What? I'm just saying." I shrugged rolling my eyes.

"Okay, let's do this differently. Rachel, I'm a witch."

I couldn't help but laugh. I mean, come on, there're no such things as witches…right? "You mean like hocus-pocus and abracadabra witch?"

"No, Rachel. I mean like "stop laughing or I'll turn you into a toad" witch," she said pouting.

"Okay, okay…I'm sorry. So can you do anything?" I said, trying to backtrack. I wanted to be supportive, but I mean, witches? Really?

"Um…watch this," she said. She jumped up and grabbed a candle. Sitting down, she closed her eyes. Not five seconds later, the candle was lit. I could tell she was mumbling something, but I couldn't make out the words.

"Whoa. Brooke, that's so cool."

I'm still not sure she could have turned me into a toad even if she had wanted to, but I'd rather not find out the hard way either. It was so difficult to keep it from her when she trusted me with something so huge—I mean, like, a giant secret—but I just couldn't force the words from my mouth. Nevertheless, I wouldn't have known where to start; so much had changed since I was four. I was fourteen then, and I didn't just see people's deaths anymore. I could see lots of things before they happened. I had seen people's abductions, their torture, and their murders. I had seen natural disasters, and some good things too, like a Christmas present or who was going to ask me to the homecoming dance.

Unfortunately, the good stuff was far and few between. I could move things with my mind, not heavy things but small ones, like a pencil or an apple. I tried to move a car once just to see what would happen. It didn't move. But how does someone tell their best friend that they can see and do these types of things? I mean being a witch was one thing, but being whatever I am, was a whole other. At least people have heard of witches.

At seventeen years old, the visions were getting worse and more frequent, and my other *gifts* were advancing as well. They appeared less like visions and more like living through it myself rather than just watching it happen. When I was upset now, objects tend to move on their own accord. I got this nagging feeling that I needed to tell someone. I'd have this sense that something bad was about to happen and I should be helping these people, but I had no clue how. I couldn't go to the police; they wouldn't believe me, and even on the slim chance that they did, I wouldn't be of much help to them. I had never met these people before, didn't know who they were, where they were from, or where they were being held. I could tell my parents, but my mom would just freak out like she usually does when I tell her something she doesn't want to hear. My dad, he would probably just tell me to embrace the visions like he did when I was little. The problem with that was, as the visions got more intense, so does the pain. It started out with just minor headaches; however, now it had progressed to nose bleeds, and the visions seem to be getting stronger every day. I sometimes feared that it was something worse than visions, like, perhaps I'm crazy or I have a tumor growing in my brain; maybe I was dropped in toxic waste as a baby. However, if it were any of those things, I would hope my parents would at least pretend to care a little more. I never got any warning before one happens, and it was getting more and more difficult to hide. More times than not, I felt like I was on the brink of death.

Some of the things I see in my visions, I know can't be true. Monsters don't exist; they are scary stories told to children to frighten them. However, in my visions, they are real—vampires, werewolves, and shape-shifters are the common ones I had come to know to be real. I wish they were extremely hot guys. Perhaps if they sparkled in the sun like in the movies, it would make it easier, but I wasn't so lucky; the things that I saw were terrifying. These things were scary, tall, dark, and sinister. The vampire I most frequently saw in my visions was skinny with sunken eyes and ash-white, almost-see-through skin, with dark hair and eyes that looked like the swirling pits of hell, the kind of eyes you feel like your soul would get consumed by if you were to stare at them for very long.

I don't know how to tell people that I see the things from their nightmares working together to take over the world. The things these monsters say and do are frightening. I had this overwhelming feeling of doom, and I didn't know how to stop it, so I tried to ignore it. Most of the time, I'm successful. I had more difficulties suppressing the feeling at night than any other time. However, I pushed the thoughts from my mind and went on with my life the best I could like every other teenage girl.

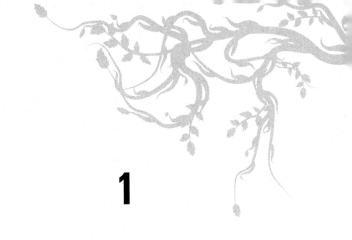

1

It was a cold and rainy night in March. I just left my best friend Brooke Middle's house where we were watching movies, and I was walking home. I wish I had driven; I only lived a couple of blocks away, so I hadn't seen the point earlier, but it was raining pretty hard now and getting colder. I shivered and wrapped my jacket around me tighter as I started to jog toward my house. My parents were out of town as they usually were; they took over running an oil company my mom's dad had owned before he died. Due to this, they were generally out of town, and I wasn't exactly looking forward to being in that big house alone.

It is an exceptionally beautiful house constructed of gray brick. It's a large two-story with a heated pool on about five acres of land. On the first floor, there's the kitchen, formal dining, breakfast nook, living room, den, my dad's study, a small gym, and a huge sunroom. The second floor consists of the master bed and bath, my room, two guest rooms, two bathrooms, a game room, and my mom's study. Still, it was better than staying at Brooke's house. Brooke was one of six children with all her siblings being younger than her. It didn't seem to matter what her mom did; that place was like a madhouse.

I could see my porch light from where I was. *Only a block to go,* I tried to comfort myself. That was when a sudden jolt of fear shot through my body like electricity. I struggled to breathe. I couldn't explain it—the uncontrollable fear that was pulsing through my veins. I felt as though I was being watched, like there was someone or something right behind me. *Oh man, Rachel, you've been watching too many scary movies,* I told myself. At that moment, a voice deep inside me begged me to run, and I just couldn't ignore it. I took off full sprint for my front door. Somewhere in the back of my mind, I was aware of the fact that if any of my neighbors saw me, they would think I had finally lost my mind. However, I couldn't ignore the fear pulsing in my veins. I was so close I could feel the doorknob in my hand. I prayed that it was my imagination and not one of my visions coming to get me. That's when I heard it—a laugh was coming from behind me. Out of instinct, I guess, I stopped and turned around to see who was laughing, but I saw no one. I took an enormous gulp of air, held it, and reached toward the gate.

I heard the laugh again. *Man, my imagination is good,* I told myself, trying to ignore it this time and opening the gate. All I wanted was to be in the warm comfort of my home safe from whatever was after me. When I turned to shut the gate, I felt it—arms wrapping around my waist from behind. That's all it took I lost it! This wasn't my imagination anymore! I screamed as loud as I could for as long as I could when one of the arms let go to cover my mouth. The laughter was louder now, almost a roar. I was starting to gasp for air when the arms finally released their hold on me!

"Man, Rachel, what were you and Brooke doing tonight? Trading ghost stories?" a male voice asked, a voice I thought I should recognize, but at this point it was hard to hear anything over the pounding of my own heart. I thought I was done for. Thanks to my visions, I was left feeling like it was only a matter of time before they would come for me. I spun quickly to see the monster that had held me. Fear, pain, and embarrassment overwhelmed me when I saw him. He was just standing there, like a five-year-old on Christmas morning, looking proud of himself.

"Luke Edger Rockwell, what in the hell is wrong with you?" I screamed, still shaken and embarrassed.

"Me? What's wrong with me? What's wrong with *you*? You knew I was coming over when you got back from Brooke's."

He was right. I did know that, granted I had forgotten until this moment.

"Well, that doesn't give you any reason to try and scare me to death!"

"Sheesh, Rachel. I wasn't trying to scare you. You could hear me laughing. I had been following you since you left Brooke's house."

"You were following me?" I interrupted, feeling rage burning in my cheeks. "Why were you following me? What gives you the right? Why didn't you say something?"

"Calm down, Rachel! I saw what kind of night it was turning out to be, and I got worried. I just wanted to make sure you were okay."

"So what? You thought you'd come over here and what? Scare the crap out of me? Yeah, that'll teach me not to be frightened the next time I have to walk home alone. Good job!" I cut him off, yelling again.

I turned my back on him and fumbled with my keys to get the door unlocked. *Great! Now I'm one of those cliché girls from the movies, the one who gets angry and can't do anything. Awesome*, I thought doing a little cheer in my head. I hated being mad at him. I knew where he was coming from, and I knew that he didn't intend to scare me. I was just so angry; nobody likes being scared, and I think I hate it more than most. All he had to do was say something. *I mean, how hard is it to say, "Hey, I'm here"? See, not that hard*, I thought, getting lost in my head. I probably wouldn't have been as angry if it hadn't been for my visions; I really had thought that they had finally come for me. I knew somewhere deep down in my soul that it was only a matter of time before my nightmares came to life. I hate being scared, especially when I have to sleep in this big house alone, and he knew it.

"Rachel, I'm...I'm sorry I didn't mean to scare you. Honestly, I was just going to pop out and say, 'Boo!' and then offer to walk you home. But you should've seen it, the sudden fear on your face. I couldn't help it. It was so funny, but when I laughed, you freaked out. Of course once it was started, there was no going back."

"Good night, Luke" I protested while walking inside.

"Come on, Rachel, let me stay, at least for a little while. You know you're going to be completely freaking out if you're alone!"

I gave him a snarl and held the door open; he quickly slid inside. Smart guy, he didn't give me a chance to change my mind; I hate when men manage to use logic against me. I shut the door behind me and locked it. I sat my bags down and went to the kitchen to get a drink. Luke followed right behind me like a puppy that had just been scolded. I shook my head, chuckling silently at him. I know I can never stay mad at him for long, nor did I ever want to for that matter. The way he looked at me when he even thought I was upset with him was heartbreaking. He would conjure up the biggest blue puppy-dog eyes; in the slim chance they didn't start to work, immediately his bottom lip would slowly begin to quiver.

He pulled out a bar stool and sat down as I went to the fridge and poured two glasses of orange juice. The inside of my parent's house was pristine, all stainless steel and cherry wood. They spared no expense when it came to their home. Although I enjoyed it, I didn't comprehend why they spent all this money on a house they weren't even around most of the time to enjoy.

"So…" he drawled, trying to break the silence.

"What, Luke?" The words slipped through my lips like venom, leaving a bitter taste behind. I was angry; my pulse was still pounding from being scared. I hated this; too often, I felt like I lived in a constant state of panic, and it was all because of my stupid visions. I just wish I knew why I had them or how to make them go away or what I was supposed to do with them for that matter.

"Rachel, I'm sorry! What more do you want me to say? Do you want me to beg? You know I will if it will make you feel any better."

"No, nothing. Look, I know you didn't mean to frighten me," I admitted in a defeated huff. "But, Luke, you scared the crap out of me."

I took a deep breath and turned to wash our glasses. I needed some space before I worked myself up again. I knew me being angry over something so stupid would only leave me feeling crummy and him with hurt feelings. I never was great at controlling my temper. Before I could start the water, he was behind me with his arms wrapped around my waist. He pulled me so tight to his chest; I could feel the rise and fall of his breathing and the beat of his heart against my back as he trailed kisses down from my ear along my bare neck.

"I really am sorry I scared you, my sweet," he whispered against my neck, sending chills throughout my body.

Ugh...that boy...if he only knew what effects his touch had on me. Standing there with his arms wrapped around my waist, I could feel his warm breath on my neck; instantly all the fear and anger melted away and was replaced by something much more powerful. As if all of this was really necessary, I swear the sheer sight of him and those big blue eyes made me weak in the knees. Luke was gorgeous, six feet tall, with light-brown spiked hair, blue eyes, and abs I could wash my clothes on. With a sigh, I turned in his arms and stared into his crystal-clear blue eyes. They truly were hypnotic. At times like these, I swear he could ask me to commit murder and I wouldn't think twice about it, just for one more minute with him and his eyes...oh, and those abs. I smiled to myself.

"Prove it!" I taunted with a witty smile and a wink.

For an average blue-blooded American boy, that would have been it, enough said, straight upstairs to bed. But, no, not with Luke. He had morals or something. He always told me, once two people became that close to one another, everything changes. The people, their relationship, everything. And he didn't want to change anything when everything was already so perfect. I suspected that there was more to it than that, but I never pushed him. I figured he would tell me when he was ready, and in the meantime, it made my parents love him all the more. Besides, as much as I hate to admit it, I did respect him for it. It was nice knowing that he wanted me for just me and not something that I could give him or make him feel.

"I'll tell you what, I'll stay awake, hold you all night, and make sure that the bogeyman doesn't get you. How does that sound?" he bargained in an extremely sarcastic tone. I swear, if he weren't the love of my life, I might just strangle him. Sometimes that boy just has a way of getting under my skin.

"Why don't you go on up to my room and change out of your wet clothes. I'm going to go take a quick shower," I told him as I walked upstairs to the bathroom. Luke stayed at my house often enough that he always left clothes here so he didn't have to worry about bringing any.

I turned on the shower and started getting ready for bed. I brushed my teeth, undressed, and stepped into my nice hot shower.

"Aaaaah!" I shrieked at the top of my lungs as frigid cold water pelted my back causing instant goose bumps to form.

Thud, thud, thud. I could hear Luke running to me from my bedroom. *Great,* I thought. *He really is going to laugh at me now.*

"Rachel, baby, are you okay?"

"Just go away," I begged, feeling utterly stupid. I quickly jumped out of the shower. I hadn't realized that he had already made it into the bathroom until he grabbed me.

Jesus, he's fast. He quickly turned me toward him in one swift movement staring into my eyes. He looked positively eatable in his low-slung pajama pants and no shirt. I could spend hours just staring at his body.

"Baby, are you okay?" he asked again with worry in his voice until he saw me staring. "See something you like?" He cocked his brow at me.

God, he is so sweet, so caring, so loving, and the best part of all is we are head over heels in love with one another. But there are times that I wish he would just shut up and go away. This just happened to be one of those times. Not only was I embarrassed, but also he was holding me at arm's length while I was completely naked.

I groaned. "Yes, I'm fine. I—" I cleared my throat. "I just forgot to turn on the hot water." I hung my head in embarrassment and ignored the fact that he plainly caught me openly gawking at him.

"Mm-hmm, I see. So no bogeyman then?" he joked, waggling his eyebrows at me.

"Go away!" I said pushing him toward the door.

"Are you sure? You think you and the hot water can sort this out without me?" he asked standing in the doorway.

I wanted to strangle him. Sometimes I swear he didn't know when to shut up. Thankfully I didn't have to respond. He put his hands up and backed out of the bathroom like I was going to shoot him or something. Then again, if I had a gun, he might have been right—not that I would ever kill him…just wound. The thought brought a smile to my face as I turned on the hot water and got back into the shower.

I love Luke and have loved him since the first time I saw him, and I was pretty sure he knew it. We met about a year ago when his family moved here from Texas. Since that day, we have been virtually inseparable, mostly.

I finished my shower and got out. I dried off and put on my pajamas, boxer shorts, and a tank top. I brushed my hair and headed for my room. Luke was already in bed with the TV on. He was watching some type of *National Geographic* or something. It wasn't something I was interested in, so I didn't pay much attention. I smiled as I walked around and crawled into the bed. I lay next to him with my head on his chest. Hmmm. How did I get to be so lucky? A dream come true. I get to lay here next to a sweet, loving, caring, intelligent man, not to mention sexy as hell. It was surreal. I had found my prince charming when it came to Luke. He eagerly held me close and turned off the TV.

"Good night," he whispered with a kiss to my head.

I must have been sleepier than I thought because I barely heard him. I slipped swiftly into a deep slumber as my mind started swirling with pictures and memories of how we met.

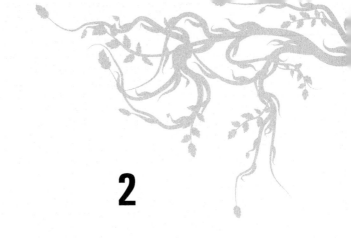

2

The first time we met actually happened quite by accident. It had been a warm summer day in July. My mom had sent me into town to pick up dinner from her favorite Italian restaurant. When I arrived at the restaurant, the food still wasn't ready, so I decided that I was going to walk to the nearby café and grab a cup of coffee.

We lived in the lovely little town of Bear Ridge. It was picture-perfect; everyone knew or at least had heard of everyone else. The town itself was to die for; it was one of those towns that just made you want to get out of your car and walk around. The storefronts were all old architecture, and the history dated back to the early 1800s. To top it off, the whole town was surrounded by trees. We weren't off any highway and didn't get that kind of traffic. We got to live in our own little world. It truly was the perfect place for a family.

I was lost in my own head as I walked down to the café. I had to have been; if I wasn't, then maybe I would have seen him standing there, but I didn't. Instead, I walked right into him, tripping over my own feet and falling to the cement in the process.

"Oh, wow, are you okay?" he asked, leaning down to help me up.

I was turning to look up at him when there was a sudden *thunk!* as our heads collided.

"Ah," I groaned reaching for my head. There was already a knot forming. I could feel my cheeks burning from the blush. *Why do these things always happen to me?*

"Sorry about that," he apologized, holding out his hand.

I graciously took his hand, allowing him to help me to my feet. I felt as though everyone in town was staring at me, laughing. I hate that feeling. I knew no one was looking, but embarrassment coursed through me just the same.

"I'm so sorry. Are you okay?" he asked once I had regained my balance.

"You're sorry. I walked into you. What do you have to be sorry about?" I didn't mean to sound as rude as I did, but I had a tendency to get angry when I was embarrassed and hurt, not that that was any excuse.

"You're right, it is your fault, and to think you haven't even apologized yet." He grinned, feeling so pleased with his response. Either that or he was flirting with me, I wasn't sure which just yet.

"I'm so sorry, really I am. I guess…I guess I was zoned out," I apologized immediately, causing my cheeks to burn hotter. At this rate, I was positive my face was going to be in a permanent state of red for the rest of my life.

"It's cool. I'm Luke," he said holding out his hand.

"Rachel. Nice to meet you," I told him, shaking his hand, and added, "I guess," as my head started to pound. I didn't realize I had hit him that hard. *This guy must have a really hard head*, I thought.

About that time, a beautiful couple walked up behind him. The woman looked to be in her early forties; she had shoulder-length blond hair and sparkling blue eyes, just like his. She was petite, not much taller than me. The man was probably my dad's age; he had darker brown hair and brown eyes, but clearly he stayed in shape. The only real signs of age that showed on either of them were a few wrinkles on their faces around their eyes and mouth.

"Oh, Rachel, it's so nice to finally meet you. I've heard so much about you," the man stated with a friendly smile.

"Finally?" I questioned with a puzzled look. Who were these people, and how do they know me? I couldn't recall ever seeing them before, and in a small town like this, that meant something. I felt something was off. The saying all parents drill into their young children started playing in my head: "Don't talk to strangers."

"Oh, I'm sorry how very rude of me. I'm Mark Rockwell, and this is my wife, Clair. It looks like you've already met one of our sons, Luke."

"Nice to meet you. How do you know me exactly?" I had no clue who these people were, and they were starting to creep me out a bit. I could feel the urge to get away from them growing in the pit of my stomach. All of my instincts were telling me to run.

"Well, you see, your father and I went to school together. We were great friends and lucky enough to stay in touch over the years. He has told me so much about you and your mother, Trish," Mark explained. "I feel like I already know you."

"Oh," was my brilliant response.

"So is your dad here? I thought we were supposed to be having dinner at your house tonight?" Mark inquired, rather confused at seeing me in town, I guess. *So that's what was going on. I should've known something was up. We don't usually get takeout unless we have guests coming over, but why hasn't anyone bothered to mention any of this to me?*

"Oh, dinner. Crap, I forgot! I was supposed to be picking it up," I stammered, suddenly remembering the reason for me coming into town in the first place. "I'm sorry. It was really nice to meet you, but I really should be getting home before my mom sends out a search party."

"It looks like you bumped your head pretty hard there, sweetie." Clair pointed out very motherly. "Why don't you let Luke drive you home since we are supposed to be there tonight for dinner anyhow?"

"Um, wow." I hesitated. "That's really sweet of you to offer, but I'm all right, really," I assured them.

I hadn't noticed that Luke was holding my arm until I turned to walk away and kind of wobbled. He quickly picked me up, grabbing the car keys out of my hand in the process. *How did he do that?*

"Hey," I tried to protest, but it was of no use. I was outnumbered.

The dizziness from my head bump was starting to set in now, and I wasn't willing to drive like this anyway. I hadn't thought I had hit it that hard. I quickly went over my options in my head. *Call Dad and have him come get me.* Nah, that wasn't a good idea. *Call Mom and have her come get me, then listen to her and all her questions all the way home.* No, thank you. *Let a complete stranger drive my car with me in it back to my home. Well, he is kind of cute. Great, now someone's cuteness is a factor in whether or not he is a psycho. God, I'm losing it.*

"I'm driving you home," he told me. Well, I guess that solves that problem. "I'll see you guys there in a little bit," he said, turning away from his parents.

Once he was sure that he had me safe inside the car—apparently, I was less of a hazard to innocent people safely seated in my car—Luke went inside the restaurant, grabbed dinner, and then drove me home. Okay, so picking me up was a little overkill. I'm pretty sure I could've walked to the car. But then again, it felt nice to be in his arms. *Wait, what?* I don't even know him. Nice to know. Apparently, when in the presence of a really cute guy, my mind goes into complete hormone mode. *Maybe I should make a note of that for future reference.* God, I really was starting to lose it. I mean, I get lost in my own head all the time, but that day with Luke was a little much even for me. It was weird he never had to ask me for directions or anything, which I guess was a good thing because my head was starting to hurt pretty bad, and I'm not sure I would be able to tell him the right way. *Then again, maybe he's a stalker*, my conscience chimed in. I did my best to ignore it. He was really cute, and I wanted so badly for him to be a good guy. It would be nice to like a good guy for a change.

Once back at my house, he helped me out of the car, allowing me to walk for myself this time while he grabbed the food.

"What took you so long?" My mother called out from somewhere in the house before we could even get all the way through the front door. My mom was a gorgeous woman—five feet five inches, thin, light-brown wavy hair, and green eyes.

"I umm...ran into some of Daddy's friends." I chuckled at how true that really was.

"Really, sweetie? Who?" my dad asked as he came out of his office to help with the food. My dad wasn't too bad-looking himself. He was tall and well built, had dark-brown hair and brown eyes and a scruffy face. The only sign of aging were the wrinkles around his eyes when he smiled. Thinking about it, him and Mr. Rockwell could be brothers. How weird.

"Good evening, Mr. Clissdale. It's so nice to see you again," Luke said, passing the food he was holding to my father.

"And you, Luke. But where are your parents?" my dad, Peter, asked.

"Oh, they'll be along shortly. Rachel bumped her head, so I drove her home."

"Err," I groaned at the mentioning of my head. I just knew my mother was going to have something to say about that; she always did. All of a sudden, my mom was standing right beside us. *Where in the hell did she come from?*

"Oh, honey, your head. What did you do? You know, Rachel, I swear, what are we going to do with you? You can't seem to do anything without hurting yourself lately."

"Gee, thanks, Mom. I think I just need some ice." I sighed as I wobbled my way to the kitchen using the walls to keep the room from spinning. I wondered if it was possible to give yourself a concussion on someone else's head.

"Well, actually, ma'am, it was my fault. I kind of bumped into her."

When I heard him say that, I spun around quickly, too quickly that I lost my balance and slid to the floor against the fridge. *Who was this guy?* He didn't even know me, and here he was, taking the blame for me running him over while he was just standing there. Where did these people come from?

"Hmm…well, Luke, would you be a dear and help Rachel to her bed while we prepare things down here for dinner? Maybe she'll feel better after lying down for a bit," my mother, Trish, asked in a very frustrated tone. *Great.* My mom's relationship and mine had always been tense; we just never were able to really bond as some mothers and daughters do. I sometimes envied other girls, the ones who went on mother-daughter dates at the spa and mall. My mom and I never did anything like that. In fact, I doubt we could even make it to the mall without trying to kill one another.

I would have argued, but to be honest, my head was hurting pretty bad at that point, and lying down sounded good. Luke didn't say a word as he came over to me, lifted me off the floor into his arms, and carried me up the stairs to my room, again without any directions whatsoever.

He lay me down while my hands gripped at my head. I was pretty sure it was going to explode. I assumed he was going to just leave me there, but he didn't. He lay down beside me playing with my hair, giving me soft kisses on my head while I whined about the pain. I should've probably felt weird about all this, seeing as how an hour ago I didn't even know him, but it all felt so right. It all seemed so perfect, like it was always supposed to be this way. I would worry about it after when my head wasn't hurting, and I could analyze it appropriately. Half an hour later, I guess we had fallen asleep, there was a loud noise, and my bed shook. Luke and I both jumped, a little confused and groggy.

"Hey, Luke, is this her?" a younger boy asked. He was tall and lanky with almost blond hair that was a little longer than Luke's, causing it to fall slightly against his forehead.

"Wow," the older one commented. He was a bear of a guy, standing probably six foot three, dark-brown curly hair, and dark-blue eyes; he looked like a football player.

I could've sworn I had seen him before, but I couldn't figure out where. I knew that there was no logical way that I had ever met him previously. I mean, I had only met the rest of his family that afternoon, and I had never left the state; I barely left this town. I didn't find it likely that I had ever run into him before. He must look like someone else. *Maybe he just has one of those faces*, I told myself, ignoring it and pushing it to the back of my mind.

"Argh, Rachel, I'm sorry, sweetie. How's your head?" Luke groaned, ignoring the guys in my room.

"Um...actually, it feels a lot better," I said, feeling very confused by this point. Who were these guys, and what were they doing in my room, on my bed? I assumed they were in some way related to Luke, but who just lets themselves into other people's bedrooms?

"Sorry about them," Luke groaned, "These idiots are my brothers, Ryan"—Luke pointed at the bear—"and Nathan. Guys, Rachel."

"Hey, nice to meet you!" they said in unison.

I couldn't actually manage to speak, so a sweet little wave was all they were getting from me.

"Nice, Luke. You've known her, what, two hours maybe, and already you're in her bed. Sweet!" Ryan gloated, holding up his hand, waiting for a high five that never came. "Oh, come on, man, don't leave me hanging. Oh, that's messed up," Ryan said, giving up on getting his high five.

I gave him my best "go to hell" look and covered my head with the blanket. *Maybe if I'm really still and quiet, they'll forget I'm here. Man, this is all just so embarrassing.*

Well, that's what you get for letting some strange guy into your bed, my conscience lectured. *First, I meet one by running into him; then I meet the other two in my room while I'm in bed with their brother. Well, this all just looks so lovely.*

"Come on, guys, the parentals sent us up here to drag you all down for dinner," Ryan said, then added, "Clothes or no clothes." He gave a quick wink to me before standing up.

With a huff, I threw the blankets off me and got out of bed. Luke was right behind me, followed by his brothers. We made our way down the stairs and into the formal dining room, where everyone was waiting.

"Nice of the two of you to finally join us," my mother said in her usual prissy sarcastic tone.

Why can't I seem to catch a break today?

"Oh, Trish, leave them alone. They're just kids," Luke's mom, Clair, defended. *Hmm...so that's what it's like to have a mom that stands up for you. Must be nice,* I thought crankily.

So dinner that night was a bit awkward, for me at least. I didn't say much, only responding to direct questions with vague answers. I listened as everyone joked and talked like old friends. It was an odd feeling having all these strangers in our home. I didn't really like it; I knew nothing about these people. The only things I knew I had managed to pick up from the conversations at dinner was that apparently the Rockwells had just moved here from somewhere in Texas. They said it was for work, but that didn't make much sense; there really wasn't work here in Bear Ridge, at least not the kind you would pack up your whole family and move for. Evidently, Ryan was the oldest, going into his junior year again this year. Luke was the middle child, the same age as me. That meant all three of us would be attending our junior and senior year together at Bear Ridge High. Nathan was the youngest at only thirteen.

I was cleaning off the table after dessert when the doorbell rang.

"Rachel, it's Adam," my dad called from the front door.

Adam? Crap, my boyfriend, I thought when I heard the name. I slowly went to the door, hoping he would quickly dematerialize or vanish before I got there. *Dang, luck wasn't on my side.* Adam was your standard good old-fashioned small-town boy. Blond hair, hazel eyes, a quarterback, well built, and dumb as a doornail. Every school has at least one, and somehow since the start of high school, I had been dating ours.

"Hey," I said as I reached the door.

"What's going on?" Adam questioned staring daggers at me. I hadn't realized that Luke was following me and now stood beside me with his hand on the small of my back. *Shit, this doesn't look good.*

"Oh, just some of my mom and dad's old friends and their kids," I informed him while stepping outside and closing the door behind me. "So, Adam, what's up? We didn't have plans tonight, did we?" I asked, knowing for a fact that we didn't because I had been avoiding him since our last big fight about a week ago. He had raised his fist to me as if he was going to hit me. Granted he quickly thought better of it, but I just wasn't interested in him after that. I had been looking for a way to break up with him for a while, and that was a great one. I just hadn't taken the time to inform him of this yet.

"Um, no. Hey, can we go for a walk?" he asked, changing the subject.

"I don't know. I really probably should get back inside. It's kind of rude of me being out here when we have company and all, ya know?" Not that I usually would have cared, but I really didn't want to be alone with him. I had had enough of Adam's crap to last me a lifetime. He was a huge flirt, and I had learned to deal with that, but I refused to put up with this new temper of his. I wasn't a punching bag, and I never would be.

"Come on, Rachel. Just come for a small walk with me. I want to talk to you," he insisted, grabbing my arm and pulling me toward the woods.

"Ow, Adam, you're hurting me," I growled at him, jerking my arm out of his grasp "Now what do you want?" I asked through clenched teeth.

"God, Rachel, why can't you just do as I ask? Why do you always have to be so stubborn and piss me off!" he yelled at me as I cautiously backed toward the door. *Holy crap, get a grip dude.*

Adam wasn't that stupid; he wouldn't do anything. Not here. Not while my dad was only a yell away…would he? I couldn't help but wonder now.

"Adam, just go—"

He didn't allow me to finish that sentence before he had me pinned to the wall using his body to block any escape I might try. Not thinking, I screamed out the first name that popped out of my mouth, "*Luke!*"

Oh, crap this isn't going to go over well, and this is why they tell you to think before you speak, my mind thought viciously at me.

Adam heard whom I yelled for, and I could see the rage burning in his eyes. Thankfully, Luke must have been listening nearby because as soon as he heard his name, he was through the door. Instantly, he grabbed my wrists, and with a quick tug, he sent me flying into his arms.

"Ryan, take Rachel inside," Luke ordered his brother, who was now standing in the doorway, quietly observing the altercation.

Man, I'm great at making first impressions, I thought sarcastically. There was no doubt in my mind by his tone of voice and stance that if I went inside, Adam may not be walking back to his car. Where there were times—okay, a lot of times—that I would've loved to see that happen, right then wasn't one of those. I just wanted him to go away, and

I wanted Luke to come back inside before I had to explain to my parents why my dad's best friend's son and my boyfriend were fighting on our front porch.

"No, Luke, come on, come inside with me. Adam, just go home, and don't bother coming back. I don't ever want to see you again," I protested.

Luke backed up, standing protectively in front of me by the door, giving Adam a look that could make one's blood run cold. He watched Adam until we couldn't make out Adam's car any longer in the distance.

Back inside, the parentals, as Ryan had put it earlier, were none the wiser to the little standoff that had just taken place outside. They were all gathered in the living room joking and talking; briefly I noticed Nathan sitting in the corner on his phone. I ran past them straight upstairs to my room; I doubt they even noticed. Luke followed me and lightly knocked on my open door when he reached it.

"Hey, can I come in?" he whispered. I gestured with my head.

He came in and sat down beside me on the bed. "Rachel, can I ask you something and you tell me the truth?"

"What?" *Well, this can't be good. This guy doesn't even know me. What could he possibly have to ask me that could upset me.*

"Is Adam the reason you have been having so many... accidents lately?"

I gave him a horrified look, wondering what exactly he thought he knew. Had Adam been hitting me? No, never. He wasn't ballsy enough to even think of hitting me. I mean, we had scrimmaged a little here and there, but then again, who didn't? We yelled and fought just like every other couple; then we kissed and made up until the next time. We were perfectly normal, or at least what I considered to be normal. Did he beat the crap out of me? No, not ever. Was I consistently getting myself hurt lately? Well yeah, but it wasn't my fault. The stupid visions made it increasingly hard not to be clumsy.

He hesitated before asking me, "Rachel, has he been hitting you?"

I had already been embarrassed and on the verge of tears, and that question didn't help at all. I burst into tears, and even in my hysteric state, I knew what Luke was going to take from it, but what was I supposed to say? *No, sorry, I'm clumsy because on a daily basis, I watch people being tortured to death in my head.* Yeah, I'm sure that would've gone over much better. I would just let him assume he knew what he was talking about, at least for now. He was going to believe he knew more than he really did. He was going to assume that I was the victim, and I hate being the victim. I could try and sort everything out, but to be honest, by this point in the night, I just didn't care anymore. So I just let him hold me while I cried. It felt nice to be in his arms.

Somewhere in the back of my mind, I was aware that this wasn't normal. You don't just meet someone and, within hours of meeting them, become this close, become this comfortable. It's not right. Those types of things are reserved for fairy tales, and I lived in anything but a fairy tale.

"Rachel, I'm sorry," he said in the most caring and loving voice I think I've ever heard. "I won't ever let anyone hurt you ever again!"

Promises, promises. I wanted to believe him, but again, this wasn't a fairy tale. It's my life, and that's simply not the way life works, despite how much I wish it would.

3

I groaned as the light from the morning sun reached my face. Instinctively, I reached for my blanket to cover my face when I heard someone snickering in my ear.

"What in the world is so funny?" I asked rolling over to face him.

"You," he said faintly. "You're just so cute."

I grunted with a disbelieving look.

"Don't you ever get tired of trying to understand our first meeting?" he asked as if my dream had been playing on a projection screen.

"How do you do that?"

"Do what?" he asked as if he didn't know exactly what I was referring to.

"Know what I'm thinking or dreaming or what I'm going to say sometimes even before I do. It's kinda freaky."

"Just a special trick I've picked up."

"No, really, Luke, tell me. What is it? Are you a witch? Vampire, maybe? Well, I guess that one doesn't make sense. I know you go out in the sun," I joked.

"Very good, oh wise one. Mmm…wise is this one, it is!" he teased while tickling me.

"Stop it! Stop it! I swear to God if you don't stop, I'm going to pee! Stop!" I screamed through my laughter and convulsions. I was actually quite violent when someone tickled me. Why they would continue to do it is beyond my comprehension.

When he finally stopped and I managed to catch my breath, I got out of bed and ran to the bathroom. I really had to pee, and it was time to start getting ready for the day anyways. After a quick shower and cereal for breakfast, Luke headed home, and I spent the next few days in a haze, thinking about the past, picking up where I had left off in my dream.

I didn't know why, but when left alone, it seemed that my mind always drifted back to the past. The past months with Luke had been different, to say the least. Things that I couldn't explain or understand had happened, things that disturbed me. I had tried not to think about them much, but it bothered me when I didn't understand something. It was like attempting to put together a puzzle when you didn't know what the picture was supposed to look like. It never helped when I tried to force them together. I would still be left just as confused and irritated as I was when I started. However, after my dream, I just couldn't help it; my mind seemed to keep wondering back there no matter what I did.

I recalled that night after everyone had left; I was lying there awake in my bed thinking about that afternoon, about Luke and his family. It was strange how they just seemed to have materialized out of the blue. They all appeared to have known my mother and me, but I knew nothing of them. In fact, I had never even heard Daddy mention them. It was very odd to suddenly have all these people want to be in my life and knowing so much about me that it was extremely lopsided. Then I thought about Luke and me. I really didn't understand the connection I felt with him. I had never felt as close to anyone as I felt to him, least of all a guy. I didn't even know him; I hadn't ever actually met him before that night. Yet I felt like I could tell him anything and everything, and scarier than that, I actually wanted to. That was what concerned me the most. I would really have to watch myself around him, make sure I didn't say anything I shouldn't. I didn't know him, which meant I couldn't trust him despite what my gut was telling me. I argued with myself for an hour before I finally decided to try and keep my distance from him and his family. It would just make things easier that way.

A week had gone by, and I was pleased with myself. I had essentially managed to stay away from Luke and his family. Not that I had given myself much time during that week to really think about it. Cheer practice had started on Monday, so I spent most of the week at the school or in the gym; and when I wasn't there, Brooke and I were hanging out. We had gone swimming, shopping, and done makeovers, it was definitely what the doctor ordered. The only hitch to my week was, regrettably, I hadn't done such a good job at avoiding Adam. He played football, so while I was at school for cheer practice, he was there for football practice. I had tried to keep my distance, but lately, Adam hadn't been in an understanding mood. It was Wednesday before he finally cornered me on the way back to the locker room.

"You know it's rude to try and ignore and avoid your boyfriend, right?" Adam had said in a harsh tone that sent shivers down my spine. I didn't even know he was there until he spoke. He came out of the shadows and moved his body so that I was pinned against the locker with him right in front of me. He used his arms to cage me in. I could feel the lockers digging into the skin of my back painfully.

"Yeah, probably a good thing I don't really care, huh?"

"Rachel, what is your issue lately? You're really acting like a bitch."

"I'm being a bitch? Well, that's rich coming from an overbearing control freak who thinks he can treat me like crap, and I'll just roll over and keep coming back for more. Get over yourself, Adam. I have," I sneered in his face, putting both my hands onto his chest and pushing him away as hard as I could. *Screw this*, I thought as I walked off.

"This isn't over, Rachel. We are meant to be, and I will have you one way or another!" he yelled and slammed his fist into the lockers where he had just had me pinned.

I didn't bother to turn and look at him. I wouldn't give him the satisfaction of knowing that he could still get to me. Thankfully, there was no one else in the hall to hear his little rant; I'm not sure I could've handled anyone knowing what was going on between us. I was pretty and popular; why should I stay with a guy who wasn't going to treat me right? I have long brown hair, green eyes the color of emeralds, I'm five feet four inches, and thin at only 110 pounds with an excellent tan.

As optimistic as my thoughts were, my real feelings betrayed me, and I felt the burning of the first tears as they left tracks down my face. I was so sick of crying over guys; they simply weren't worth it. However, it didn't stop the tears from coming. Mercifully, I didn't run into anyone while I quickly showered and changed. The last thing I wanted was to have to explain my tears to one of my friends.

As often as I told myself, he didn't matter, that what he said was only words and they couldn't hurt me. It was a lie. They did hurt, and they were starting to take their toll on me. Sometimes I wished he would just hit me and get it over with. A bruise would heal, but the pain of words all too often hurt deeper and longer than the quick and sudden pain of a punch.

After that encounter, the rest of the week flew by in a blur of cheers, angry stares from Adam, and the few moments I got with Brooke in the evenings.

———— ◆ ————

It was Saturday now, and I had just gotten out of the shower when I heard someone calling my name. I couldn't place the voice, so I grabbed my towel, hesitating by the bathroom door in an attempt at figuring out who could have possibly been in my house. It couldn't be my parents; they left on a business trip early this morning, and I would have recognized their voices, right? I would have sworn I locked all the doors before getting into the shower.

I took an enormous gulp of air and quietly tiptoed to my room. I couldn't believe it when I saw him sitting there on my bed; he scared me to death, I almost dropped my towel.

"Luke! What are you doing here?" I questioned him, feeling upset that not only did he let himself into my house but also into my bedroom. I mean, come on, where's the privacy people.

"Your dad called my dad, and my dad asked me if I would stop by and check on you while they were away," he explained as I rummaged through my closet for clothes.

"Okay, so you thought you'd come on over and break and enter. Makes sense," I said glancing over my shoulder at him.

"Whoa whoa whoa, I didn't break anything. I used the key that your dad left for me."

"He did what?" I asked, abandoning my search for clothes. When they got back, my dad and I would have a long talk about what was appropriate and what wasn't. What kind of father leaves a key for some guy to get into their house and check on his daughter? Apparently, my parents had lost their minds too. *Awesome.*

"Rachel, what's going on?" he asked surprisedly, I think, at seeing me so angry. "I thought we had gotten along great that first night, and now I haven't seen or heard from you in a week. You won't answer my calls or call me back for that matter. Did I do something to upset you?"

I sighed and sat down on my bed next to him. I leaned my head on his shoulder as I tried to explain. I didn't want him to feel bad or as though any of this was his fault. It really wasn't. It was just me attempting, poorly might I add, to sort things out. I wanted to resist the urge I was feeling to be close to him, for him to be mine, to be in his arms. I didn't wish to feel this way about anyone; I just wanted to be me. I didn't want to be that girl that needed a guy to be happy.

"I don't know. It's just that…" I sighed. "You and your family showed up out of nowhere, it seems, and you all know so much about me, which is creepy…and then there's you and me. I don't understand it, Luke. I don't even really know you, yet I can't help but want to be close to you. It scares me. None of this feels real. You don't meet someone and fall head over heels. It just doesn't happen like that in real life. I don't believe in love at first sight or any of that nonsense."

He slid up into my bed and lay down, putting his arm out for me to lie down with him. Forgetting all about still being in my towel and my decision to stay away from him, I moved up, snuggling into him with my head on his chest. This felt right; it felt like this was where I was meant to be. I wanted to be comforted, to be told everything was okay, and that what I felt was real. That I was loved, cared for, and cherished, but the logical part of my brain said he couldn't give me any of those things. How could he? He didn't even know me.

"Rachel," he said, kissing the top of my head softly as he spoke. "I'm real, I promise, and I feel the same way about you. The past week I tried my hardest to leave you alone, let you have your space, but it seemed like there was some magnetic field drawing me back to you. I can't tell you how many times I picked up the phone to call you or walked out to my car to come over and check on you and had to talk myself out of it. I don't understand these feelings any better than you do, but I also don't want to try to force them away either."

This can't be real. Fairy tales just don't exist. How could I lie there and want to believe him? How could I put my heart in jeopardy like that? Screw it! It won't hurt me to just let it be and feel for once…right? My heart wanted to believe that, but my brain was screaming it could hurt a lot, but I guess love comes at a price. I just hope it was a price I could pay. His words were so sweet; I kissed his chest and lay there in his arms, basking in the love I felt. Even if it was puppy love or fake, at that moment, it felt perfect. Maybe it was exactly what I needed. The next thing I knew I was struggling to open my eyes. I must have fallen asleep. With a stretch, I kissed his cheek.

"Mmm...what time is it?" I asked still groggy and stretching.

"Nine in the evening."

"Nine? How long have I been asleep for?"

"A little over four hours."

"I'm so sorry. Did you sleep at all, at least?"

"Nope, just watched you. You're so beautiful," he told me, holding me tight.

Okay, so kind of creepy in a very kind of romantic way, *I think*. I blushed and went to get up when I remembered I had never gotten dressed. Panic started to ensue as I frantically searched for my towel. *Where's my towel? Crap, where is it?* I thought while trying not to reveal my body. Granted seeing as I clearly didn't have it anymore and was covered up now, I'm sure he already got a good view of my goods. *Great.*

"You wiggled out of it while you were sleeping, so I moved it off the bed out of your way and covered you up. I didn't want you to get cold. I'll go downstairs and wait while you get dressed," he announced and kissed me on my cheek. He stood up and walked out the door.

"Thanks. That was really sweet of you," I replied as he shut my door behind him.

What kind of guy sees a naked chick that he likes and just covers her up? How weird, I thought as I swiftly rolled out of bed. I tossed on a pair of yoga pants and a T-shirt, ran a brush through my hair and pulled it up into a ponytail. This day was weird, and I was ready for it to be over. *I think.*

He greeted me as I got downstairs. "Oh, good you're ready to go."

"Go?" I looked at him puzzled. "Go where?"

"To my house for dinner. I figured you slept all day, you've gotta be hungry."

"Luke, it's nine o'clock at night," I protested. "Who eats dinner this late?"

"I know what time it is. Would you just come on, they're waiting for us." He pulled me toward the door. "My parents called while you were sleeping. They said to just come over whenever you woke up."

"I should change," I whined as he pushed me toward the front door.

"Stop it, you look fine," he assured me.

"Luke, stop," I said finally pulling my hand out of the death grip he had it in.

"What?"

"I at least need shoes."

"Oh. Yeah, okay. Get your shoes."

Once my shoes were on, we were in the car and on the way to his house. The ride to his house was quiet. We just listened to music. It was nice that neither of us felt we had to fill the silence with idle chitchat. I had no idea where they lived. I watched as we drove into town and back out the other side. We were about a mile outside of town when he turned into a long driveway. I gasped as his house came into view; I had never seen anything like it before. The outside was done in wood and windows. There were tons of windows. It was truly a beautiful two-story house. It made ours look like a shack by comparison.

"Wow," I finally managed to say as he opened the door for me.

"Thanks, glad you like it."

It was like straight out of a magazine. It was immaculately decorated in a contemporary style. Everything was very modern, new age, and sleek. He led me through the living room and into the dining room, where everyone was already waiting.

"Good evening, Rachel," Mark called as we entered the room. "Thank you for joining us."

"Thank you for having me, Mr. Rockwell." I blushed. He was always so formal it kinda threw me off my game. Luke pulled a chair out for me. Then he walked over and sat down next to me. I heard Ryan across from me, taunting Luke as he sat down.

"Nice you've seen her twice, slept with her twice."

"Well, I hope you're hungry," Clair told me while handing me an enormous plate of food and ignoring Ryan's comment.

"Oh, thank you, ma'am." There was so much food I had no idea how I was going to manage to eat it all.

"She likes to cook," Luke told me after reading the expression on my face. I wasn't used to this; my mom wasn't exactly what you would call a chef. Most of the time, my dad or I cooked. Weekday meals were usually my job, and he took over the weekends, seeing as how on weekends I was always in and out. It's actually pretty funny now that I think about it; if it wasn't for the two of us, I don't think she would ever eat. God only knows how she survived before us.

"Rachel, how has your week been?" Clair asked as we all started to eat.

"Uh…good, I guess. Just cheer practice and hanging with friends."

"You're a cheerleader?" Ryan asked.

"Yeah, is that a problem?"

"Nope," was all he said, giving Luke a knowing look. I had no idea what that was all about, but it left me feeling oddly jealous for some reason.

"So, Rachel, are you ready for school to start back?" Mark asked. Of course, he had to ask me the second I put food into my mouth. I quickly swallowed, hardly taking the time to chew.

"Might as well get it over with…I guess."

He chuckled. "So I take it you don't like school very much then?"

"Um…no, actually I love school. I think the curriculum could use some updating, but other than that, it's pretty great. It's the students I'm not very fond of," I answered honestly, perhaps a little too much so.

Ryan began laughing at my response. I glared at him and managed to kick him under the table.

"Ouch!" he whined as my foot struck his shin.

It was strange to me; I had only just met these people, yet when I was in their presence, I felt like family, like I was just meant to be here with them.

"Ryan, what are you complaining about now?" Clair asked in a sigh.

"Nothing, ma'am," he responded glaring at me. Suddenly there was another *thump!*

"Ryan!" Luke scolded when he got kicked this time. Ryan and I snickered, knowing that he had meant to kick me and missed. Instantly there was another *thump!*

"Luke!" Nathan complained.

Thump!

"Ouch! Hey, that's not very nice," I grunted when Nathan kicked me.

"Well, I suppose dinner is over when everyone at the table begins playing footsie," Mark lectured us.

"Sorry, sir," the four of us chanted in unison.

Everyone retired to the living room as I helped Clair bus the table and do the dishes. If I were being honest, it felt nice to be around them. My parents were away so often I had forgotten what it was like to really be a part of a family.

"Thank you, but you don't need to help me. You're our guest."

"It's the least I can do."

We were just finishing up loading the dishwasher when Luke joined us.

"So would you like the grand tour now?" he asked, holding out his hand for mine.

"Sure. Thank you for dinner, Mrs. Rockwell. It was delicious, and it was very kind of you to think of me."

Luke pulled me from the kitchen. He led me up the stairs, acknowledging everyone's rooms as we passed it. All along the walls, there were these black and white photos of landscapes; some of the pictures were truly breathtaking. I had to wonder if they had taken them or if they were just decoration. At the end of the long hall, there was a room with the door open.

"My room," he announced and led me in.

"Wow." I stated looking around. He had a flat screen, a king-size bed, a wall of DVDs and CDs, and a whole wall lined with books. I gave him a questioning look in reference to all the books. He just didn't take me as one who liked to read in his spare time.

"My dad likes to read, so he just assumes everyone else does too. My brothers have a ton as well. So what do you think? You like it?" he asked, flopping down onto the bed.

"Very nice," I said as he reached over to the nightstand, grabbing a remote.

"Would you like to watch a movie?" he asked. Before I could respond, there was a knock on the door.

"Put your clothes back on, we're coming in," Ryan told us as Nathan and he walked in.

"Sheesh, you could've at least given us time to take them off," Luke teased.

I smacked him on the arm, blushing. I couldn't believe he just said that. He looked at me with apologetic eyes.

"You staying over tonight?" Ryan asked me.

"Umm…" I said, looking at Luke as he nodded. "Well, I guess so then."

"Eek…a slumber party," Ryan exclaimed, shaking his hands like a little girl and jumping onto the bed between Luke and I. Nathan just stood quietly by the door, watching as his older brothers made fools of themselves.

"Yeah, we thought we would start off with a romantic movie followed by lots of cuddles," Luke indicated as he grabbed Ryan, snuggling up to him real close.

"Ya know, this wouldn't be so bad if you were Rachel," Ryan taunted.

"In your dreams, big boy." I retorted. "I think Nathan and I should go play a game or something and leave you two love birds alone."

"Hey, don't drag me into this," Nathan said from the door, shaking his head and causing me to pout.

"Well, I can see where I'm not welcome," Ryan whined, getting up and walking over to Nathan. "Come on, Nateypooh. We can have our own slumber party." He put his arm around Nathan's shoulder and led him out of the room while Nathan stared down at the floor. I'm pretty sure his face was red, but I couldn't get a good-enough look to be sure.

Luke got up and shut the door behind them, locking it this time. As I got up and started going through his dresser drawers. If I was staying here tonight, I wanted to be as comfortable as possible. I would've been just as happy to go back home. I wasn't sure I was ready for all this—not just the Luke thing, but any of it. His family seemed to be really close, and it was awesome, but I wasn't sure I was ready to be one of them.

"What are you looking for?" he asked, turning around.

"Nothing. I found it." I pulled out a pair of boxers. "Turn around." I quickly yanked off my clothes, threw on his, and jumped into bed.

"Comfy?" he asked as he walked back to the bed. He stripped down to his boxers and pulled on a pair of pajama pants before climbing in.

"Yup," I said popping the *p*.

We got settled in, and he pushed a button on the remote. The lights turned off, and soft music started playing. It was unbelievable; like a dream, little stars twinkled on the ceiling. I had to get one of those things for my room. It was so cool. I knew after sleeping all afternoon I shouldn't be tired; it must have been the music. I felt as though I had just closed my eyes when the sun coming in through the windows woke me. I stretched and reached for Luke, but he wasn't there. I could smell bacon and eggs cooking downstairs. So I quietly rolled out of bed and headed down. As I reached the landing, I heard Luke call out to me.

"Well, good morning, sunshine," he said walking up.

"Mmm...good morning," I answered, wrapping my arms around his neck and kissing him. Apparently, all my fears went away in the night—either that or my brain wasn't awake yet. Either way, it seemed I was along for the ride. He quickly picked me up, forcing me to wrap my legs around his waist, and walked into the dining room while kissing me. He shifted all my weight to one arm and used his other to pull out a chair for me. *Damn, he's strong. I can barely do that when I'm babysitting Katie, and she's only five.* He sat me down and put a napkin in my lap.

He leaned down to me, softly whispering into my ear. "How do you like your eggs?"

"Mm...over medium please." I had been so absorbed in our own little bubble that I hadn't noticed the rest of his family already sitting around the table. *Man, I have got to learn to quit zoning out.*

"Good morning, Rachel. Did you sleep well?" Clair asked as I slumped down into my chair, embarrassed, hoping the world would suddenly open up and swallow me whole. What kind of parents are okay with their son acting this way with a girl he just met?

"Probably, if they slept," Ryan advised before I even had the chance to process everything.

I could feel the embarrassment burning at my cheeks. "Aw, that's so cute. You're jealous of your little brother," I retorted in a grumble.

Everyone seemed to have gotten a good laugh out of my comment—everyone except for Ryan, that is, who sat there staring at me with blazing eyes.

"Your breakfast, beautiful," Luke said, setting a plate in front of me a few minutes later.

"Thanks. It smells great," I assured him. "Thank you for allowing me to stay, Mr. and Mrs. Rockwell. It was a pleasant change to always having to stay alone."

"You know you're more than welcome here anytime you like," Mr. Rockwell informed me.

"Thank you, both. That's very kind of you." We all finished breakfast, and I helped Luke clean up afterward.

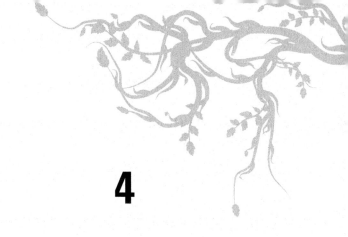

4

"**S**o I thought we'd spend the day together if you like," Luke mentioned as we finished doing the last few dishes.

"That actually sounds like a lot of fun," I said as we wiped our hands.

We went upstairs and grabbed the clothes from the night before. I didn't bother changing back into my clothes. As soon as we were finally alone in the car, I turned to him. "What the hell was up with picking me up and carrying me into the kitchen?"

"Huh?" he looked at me, totally puzzled.

"This morning you carried me from the stairs to the table."

"Yeah, so?"

"So…what the hell, man? Your whole family was there. It was so embarrassing."

"Why? They didn't think anything of it."

"Really, Luke? Are you that dense? Sheesh, it was embarrassing because, for starters, we barely know each other, and since last night, we've been acting as though we've known each other our whole lives. Secondly, now your parents are going to think we are screwing, and I prefer them to know me a little better than they do before they start to think I'm a total slut. And why wouldn't they think anything of it? Is this normal behavior for you with girls you've just met?"

"Wow, Rachel, chill, no one thinks you're a slut. I promise, no one in my family thought anything of it." *Right.*

"But why didn't they think anything of it, Luke?" I asked, getting angry. We hadn't had the ex's talk, and I was not sure I wanted to. Granted seeing as how he hadn't really put the moves on me yet, I was under the impression that he was a virgin.

"Look, Rachel, they just didn't, okay? My parents have three boys. They have come to expect certain things and just don't think anything of it."

With a huff, I sat back in my seat and let it go. I wasn't going to win anyways. The rest of the drive back to my house was quiet. We just sat listening to music. I thought about what I was doing, what I was thinking. It's not like me to allow myself to become so consumed with emotions. I had learned at an early age that things like that only lead to pain and confusion. We were pulling into my driveway when I gasped.

"What? Who? Why?" I stammered looking around my yard. Someone had TP'ed and egged my house during the night.

We got out of the car and walked slowly toward the door. When I saw Adam sitting there on my front porch. The nerve of him to do this and then wait for me.

"Adam! Why? What were you thinking?" I shouted in anger.

I didn't comprehend what was going on. Adam had been a whole other person when we met. He was kind, smart, funny, a good listener, always there to talk to, and so full of life. Only in the past few months had all of that changed. He turned into some kind of monster, and he treated me as if I were his sworn enemy. It appeared as though he wanted so desperately to kill me but couldn't. However, he didn't seem content to leave me alone either.

"I told you, Rachel, you...are...*mine*. You can delude yourself otherwise by hanging out with this freak, but make no mistake about it. You will be mine again, whether you like it or not," Adam growled and stormed off.

I stood there for probably five minutes with my mouth gaping. *I will be his, my ass. Does he even hear himself? What kind of person says those things? What the hell is his issue? What in the world did I do?*

Luke and I exchanged confused looks before going inside. He waited downstairs for me while I ran up to quickly get into the shower.

What was he thinking? Why would he do this? Why sit here and wait for me to come home before leaving? What could've happened to him to cause him to become so different from the Adam I used to know? And what the hell did he mean by whether I like it or not? You can't just decide that another human being is your property. The world doesn't work like that. Maybe it's me that doesn't know the way the world works, I pondered while I was in my shower. When the day had started I felt on top of the world, so happy, so loved, all of that was gone now; the only things that remained were pain and confusion. After I had finished with my shower, I got dressed and headed back downstairs.

"Well, I guess I might as well start getting all this cleaned up. The last thing I need is for my parents to come back and see it," I said, indicating to the mess Adam had so generously left for me.

"Yeah. Do you want some help?" Luke suddenly seemed shy. I knew I was pissed, but I didn't think it showed enough for him to sound like that.

"That's really sweet of you, but you don't need to help. You should go enjoy your day. Why should you be stuck here with me helping me clean up the mess that my ex made."

"It's going to take you forever to clean all of that up on your own. In fact, why don't I call my brothers, and with all of us, it will be as good as new in no time at all."

"That's really sweet, and if you want to stay, I'm not going to stop you, but I really don't want your brothers here. Okay?" *The last thing I wanted right now was more people knowing what kind of jerk I had been dating. I felt so embarrassed that I had ever even been associated with a person like that, let alone dated him.*

"Sure. Are you all right?"

"Yes…no…maybe?" I shrugged.

"Do you want to talk about it?"

"I don't know, Luke. I mean isn't there a rule 'no talking about exes with the new person you like'?" I joked.

"Hmm. Nope, never heard that rule." Luke smiled. "You know, I want to be your friend too, but you have to let me in, and talking with me is a good start."

I sighed as I headed to grab some trash bags. I was going nuts trying to figure all this stuff out on my own. I knew I needed to talk to someone about it, and where I would usually just call Brooke, Luke was already here, and they say that the best relationships are built on trust and communication, right? But where do I even begin?

"You ready to get started?" I asked returning to the front door. He nodded and followed me out the door. Once in the front yard, I turned back and stared at the house.

"Oh my god. Does that say *bitch*?"

Apparently when we first walked up, we missed the extent Adam had gone through. He had written *bitch* and *slut* all over my windows in shaving cream.

"What the hell is his problem? I mean he was never like this when we first got together. He was so sweet, like a real gentleman. Do you know he used to even hold doors open for me and carry my books and bags? Now I don't know. He's been this way for a while now. It was like he went to bed one night and woke up the next morning and was like, 'Hey, you know what might be fun? Let's treat Rachel like shit. Yeah, that'll be fun.' I mean, who does this?" I'm not sure I had meant to say all of that, but once my mouth was open, it just all came pouring out.

"Rachel, I'm sorry. I don't know why he's acting like this, but I could kick his ass if it'd make you feel any better."

I smiled at him. "That's really sweet, but I can handle Adam on my own." I shook my head and started to work on cleaning up. I didn't know what else to say I'm sure I could have set there and ranted all day, but I just didn't want to. I was beyond angry, and if I weren't careful, I would end up taking it out on Luke.

Luke helped me clean everything up, then headed home. I went back inside myself and took another shower. After my shower, I finally made the time to call Brooke. I needed my best friend. It wasn't five minutes after I called her that she was walking through my front door.

"Okay, I'm here. I have my jammies, rocky road ice cream, and *Magic Mike*. So what's going on?"

God, I loved her so much; she knew exactly how to cheer me up. We spent the night bashing guys and wishing we could have a guy like Channing Tatum. Six o'clock came very early, considering we didn't go to sleep till 3:00 a.m. Unfortunately,

I had cheer practice and had to get up. I laid in bed for at least twenty minutes, seriously considering skipping. Regrettably, I knew I couldn't, so eventually I did get up and get dressed. I left Brooke sleeping and headed to school.

When I got back that afternoon, Brooke had already left. I quickly made my way up the stairs and into a nice, hot relaxing bath. The next three days, I spent mostly in my room except when I had practice. Thank God for Luke; if he hadn't been taking care of me, I don't think I would have eaten. I spent the days attempting to understand my "perfect life."

Two weeks ago, it had been perfect, or so I thought. I had a boyfriend, granted he was acting like a jerk (but most teenage boys usually were), a beautiful house, a car I loved, and I was pretty and popular. I couldn't make sense of Adam lately. When we first became friends in the fifth grade, he was an entirely different person. I wasn't delusional. I knew I wasn't the same as I was then, but I wasn't acting psychotic like he was either. He changed into this person I couldn't even recognize. He became controlling, possessive, mean, and aggressive. I just wanted everything to go back to normal. I wish I could go back to fifth grade when everything was simple and easy. What would make a guy change so drastically so quickly?

As if I didn't have enough to figure out with Adam, I was still trying to figure out Luke and me as well. How did he always seem to know what I was going to say? Why was there this pull? I had never felt anything like it before in my life. I had had crushes and liked guys before, but never had I ever felt like I had to be near them, had to talk to them. It was strange and, to be honest, a little frightening, especially since I didn't even really know who he was. However, when he was near, it was like all the things that were bothering me melted away; all the stress and crap were just gone, and the only thing that mattered was him.

My parents had just gotten home; I could hear them downstairs talking with Luke. He was just leaving when they got here; he had brought me dinner. He must have told them something because no one bothered me, but I knew it couldn't have been the truth since they would've been in my room quicker than I could blink. I would have to ask him what he told them, so if asked, I could keep my story straight. As much as I dislike my parents at times, that's the one thing they've always been good at, protecting me no matter what the threat.

The next morning, I got up and slowly started getting ready; it was the first day of school. *Oh joy.* I took a shower, brushed my teeth, washed my face, blow dried my hair, got dressed, and did my makeup. I was just about to walk out the front door when my dad called out to me.

"Have a good first-day, sweetie."

"Thanks, Daddy. See you later."

I'm not sure why, but even with all the traveling my parents did, all the time, they still made a point to always be home on the first and last day of school. It made me smile; it was something so small, but it was enough of a reminder at just how much they loved me.

Walking out to my car, I tossed my bag into the back seat and headed for Brooke's house. I always enjoyed the first days of school. Learning the new schedule, seeing all your friends, hearing how everyone's summer went, and just the smell of the school itself put me into a good mood. I don't know, it's just fun to me, and I could use a little fun right now. For the first time in a week, I had no thoughts of Adam or Luke, and to be honest, it felt so nice not having any worries about boys or drama.

"Hey, girl, you ready for yet another year?" very chipper, I asked as Brooke got into the car.

"If I have to be."

Brooke wasn't as popular as me. She was beautiful with her red curly hair, hazel eyes, and thin figure. She and her family were really close, and she just didn't seem to truly fit in at school. Granted she and I had been best friends since she first moved here in the first grade.

"Well, I think this year is going to rock."

"That's easy for you to say. You're head cheerleader, a straight As student, on the student body council, and all the teachers and students love you. You have your quarterback boyfriend and every other guy drooling over you."

"Wow, make me sound like some freak of nature, why don't you, and I told you I'm not seeing Adam anymore."

"Right...Look, I know the two of you are on the outs right now, but you guys will make up. You always do. Then the two of you will be back to making out under the bleachers in no time. You two are meant for each other."

"What's that supposed to mean? You think I deserve the way he treats me?"

"That's not what I said. I was just saying your head cheerleader, he's quarterback, both of you come from well-to-do families. I don't know, Rachel. It's just always been the two of you."

"Yeah, well, things change," I told her as we pulled up at school.

Our usual group was waiting for us in front of the school—Ashley, a pretty blonde; Melissa, a geeky brunette; and Samantha, the next most popular girl in school. Sam had always wanted to be me and was jealous of everything I had, and to be honest, we couldn't stand each other, but hey, that's high school. Your worst enemies are suddenly your best friends.

"Hey, ready for a new year?" Ashley greeted us as we walked up.

"Well, ready or not, here we are." I laughed. We all sat down at one of the picnic tables in front of the school. We pulled out our schedules to compare them like we always did on the first day.

"Oh, yuck, I have Ms. Brady for English first thing," said Sam.

"Me too."

"So do I."

"Yup."

"Well, at least we all have one class together," I said as we got up and headed to our lockers. We were laughing and talking as we went and sat down for our first class.

Rachel Clissdale Class Schedule

Block A
1st period—Ms. Brady, English
2nd period—Mr. King, Modern World History
Lunch
3rd period—Mr. Clark, Precalculus
4th period—Ms. Bree, Gym
Block B
5th period—Mrs. Krauss, Biology
6th period—Ms. Garza, Spanish
Lunch
7th period—Mr. Bates, Chemistry
8th period—Mr. Lenard, Physics

"All right, everyone. Quiet down," Ms. Brady said.

And yet another year begins, I thought.

Ms. Brady was an old woman who probably had too many cats. She was way to passionate about English and loved to suck the pleasure out of her students. She had gray hair, which was always in a bun, and thick glasses.

"All right, we all know the usual speech. Read your syllabus, and you won't have to ask me any questions about what is going on. To make myself clear, everything that is expected of you this year to pass this class is in your syllabus. *So read it*."

I looked over to Brooke and mouthed, "Blah, blah, blah," using my hand to mimic the mouth. Brooke, Sam, Ashley, and Melissa all broke out laughing. Unfortunately, we heard Ms. Brady stop midsentence, and I didn't have to turn around to know she was staring at us.

"Well, since some of us don't care what I have to say and are apparently bored, perhaps the five of you would prefer a pop quiz over one of your summer reading assignments. Everyone clear off your desks, mouths shut, eyes forward."

An hour later, we were finally free.

"Thank God that's over," Brooke said.

"Yeah, what a hag," agreed Sam. "I mean, all that just for laughing."

"Did anyone actually do the summer reading?" Melissa asked with a slight blush to her pale cheeks.

"Well, we all know Rachel did," Ashley joked.

I stuck my tongue out, not giving them the satisfaction of hearing me say yes. "Well, I've got to get to history. Yay. See you all at lunch."

I didn't feel the need to justify them with a response. My friends knew me well enough to know that not only had I done the summer reading but I had also done all the summer recommended homework as well.

The day went by pretty quickly after that, and it was time for lunch before I knew it. So far, I had managed not to run into Adam or Luke, which I was grateful for. Not that I would have minded seeing Luke. I really wouldn't have, but the person he knew me to be isn't the person I am at school. At home, I get to be me, fun and playful, but at school I am rather mean and bitchy. What can I say, I'm one of the popular ones. However, I knew by lunch my luck would run out. I fought my urge to skip lunch and spend the time in the library just to avoid the scene that I knew was coming with Adam. I was done fighting; it was the first day of school, and I was ready for everything to get back to normal. Unfortunately, I had a feeling that was never going to happen, so begrudgingly, I headed to lunch.

My friends and I had just sat down with our lunches when there was a sudden commotion. None of us had to look up to know that that meant the jocks had finally joined the lunchroom. Sadly, I also knew that meant another more public fight with Adam was soon to come. I no sooner thought it than I heard.

"Rachel? Aren't you going to come eat with me? I don't seem to see your new toy anywhere? Better warn him you like to break hearts."

"Oh, shut it, Adam. I didn't break your heart, and you know it. Do you even have one?" I could hear the oohs and aahs around the lunchroom. I was just about to get up and leave as I didn't need this crap when someone touched my shoulder; I looked up to see Luke pulling a chair over to sit down with us. I wasn't prepared for the huge smile that graced my face just by the sheer sight of him.

"Speak of the devil, and he shall appear. So, Luke, how is my girlfriend treating you?" Adam taunted from across the room. "Has she showed you that little thing she likes to do with her tongue yet?"

I had just opened my mouth to respond when Luke whispered, "Just ignore him. He's only trying to get a rise out of you."

"Well, it's working," I whispered back harshly. I was sick of this. Why couldn't he just get over it and do what every other dumped guy does? Sleep with a ton of other girls and try to make me jealous, I could deal with that.

"That bad, huh? Can't say I'm surprised. Looks like you can't keep any man happy for very long, huh, Rachel?" Adam taunted again.

Unfortunately my inability to control my tongue and temper made another appearance. That was it, I was going to end this once and for all. I was not sure I actually made the conscious decision to go over there, but before I knew what I was doing, I was on the other side of the lunchroom leaning into Adam and whispering in his ear, "You know, you never do know when to shut up. The only one you are embarrassing is you. You should really learn to let it go, Adam. It's really starting to get sad and desperate. Plus Luke knows a lot more about what I can do with my tongue than you ever will." I taunted him back, giving him a quick kiss on the cheek.

To all the other people in the lunchroom, it looked like a familiar sight, me giving Adam our usual kiss on the cheek. I winked at the other jocks as I pulled back and walked away. I went and sat back at my table and introduced the girls to Luke. I refused to let Adam get to me anymore. There was a clear look of intrigue on all my friends' faces as I sat back down. However, it was none of their business what I had just said to Adam, and I didn't feel like sharing, especially with Luke here.

It took all ten seconds after introducing Luke before Sam was all over him, hitting on him. I felt sorry for Luke; he looked like a lost puppy when Sam happily got up and moved around the table squeezing between him and Melissa. She was leaning into him so much that she had practically crawled into his lap. I could tell by the look on Sam's face that she wasn't happy when her advances went unnoticed by Luke. She had always tried to take my boyfriends away from me, not that it ever worked, and Luke was easily the hottest guy in school, so why should he be any different? I knew that Luke wanted to ask what was up with me. He had this constant look of questioning on his face, but it's not like I could explain even if I wanted to, which I really didn't. What would I say even if I did? "Oh, hey, sorry about that. I have to be a bitch at school." Yup, that's not going to happen. I always hated school politics. I hated that to be popular I had to be a bitch. I really didn't like to be mean to people. But then there were people like Sam, who just brought out the worst in me, or maybe that's just what I told myself to be able to sleep at night.

Conversation flowed easily after that, and it was time to go back to class before I was really ready. By the grace of God, Adam didn't say anything else to us for the rest of lunch. I said good-bye to Luke and the other girls as Sam and I headed to our next class.

"I hate precal. I don't even know why we have to take it. I mean, hello, it's called a calculator and Google," Sam whined.

"Yeah, but unfortunately, we don't have a choice." I would know, I tried everything to get out of it. I hated math in all forms. However, I was "gifted," as I kept being told, and good at everything, unlike Sam.

"So, Luke is cute. Are you guys like a thing?"

I knew Sam was going to bring this up, but I didn't know what to say to her. *Were we a thing?* I don't know, but I didn't want her to have him, and it's not like it really mattered what I said. If Sam wanted him, she was going to go after him no matter what I said.

"I don't know. Right now, we are just friends...I think."

"Oh, good, so he's like available then," Sam said with a huge smile. I didn't justify her with a response. She was going to do what she wanted whether we were a thing or not.

"You know, Adam is single now. I know how much you wanted him last year." I knew by saying this I was rattling her cage, but I just didn't seem to care anymore. I was sick of her trying to get what I already had.

"Ew, and take your leftovers. No, thank you."

I just laughed and shook my head at her. I didn't even know how to respond to that. *So they're my leftovers when I'm done with them, but not while I'm still with them? How does that make any sense?* Sometimes I wondered what it must be like inside her mind.

We headed into class, found two seats, and sat down right as Mr. Clark stood up to start today's lecture. The first day of school was such a joke in terms of classes. It's not like we were going to learn anything on the first day of school. I didn't understand why we had to sit through this so many times. It was the standard lecture. "Okay, class you are going to need blah, blah, blah... I expect from you...and so forth and so on." After your first year, you basically had the speech down and didn't need to listen. Sam and I played hangman and talked while Mr. Clark continued his tired old speech. Thankfully he wasn't as crotchety as Ms. Brady, and there were no pop quizzes.

"So where were you all vacation?" I asked Sam. It wasn't two days after school let out that she had seemingly vanished without a word to any of her so-called friends.

"God, Rachel, I wasn't on vacation. I was on holiday," she said sounding as if I had offended her.

"Okay...and what's the difference exactly?"

"Well, here in America we call it vacation, but I wasn't in America. I was in London, and there they call it holiday... duh."

How the hell was I supposed to know that?

Apparently, the reason Sam had been missing all summer was that she had convinced her parents to let her go stay in London with a friend. Luckily for her, they didn't speak a foreign language there because Sam failed French last year and Spanish the year before that. What her parents didn't know according to Sam was that said friend was some guy. As much as I wish I could think she was lying, for the safety of it, I knew Sam all too well by now and knew that she was most likely telling the truth. I mean who in their right mind goes halfway around the world to meet some guy they met on the Internet. I've tried really hard to understand where she was coming from, but I just couldn't. It was like she had no self-preservation at all. If the guy was even a little cute, had money, or was interested in someone other than Sam, she just had to have him. It didn't have to be all three; any of the three would do. She would use him for a little while, get bored, and then throw him away like a used tampon.

Mercifully, class was over, and we were headed in separate ways again. Sam was a friend but only because we were the two most popular girls in school. It really was more of a love/hate relationship. We hated each other, but in high school, thy enemy is thy best friend. To be honest, I couldn't be left alone with her for too long before I started contemplating all the ways she could choke on her own tongue while talking. I only had one class left, then off to cheer practice.

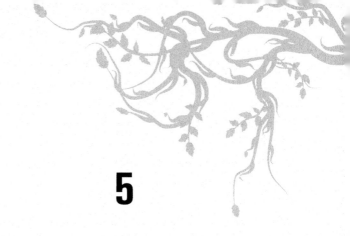

5

I was exhausted by the time I got home. It always took a little bit to get back into the routine of things, and everything going on with Adam and Luke wasn't helping at all. I took a quick shower, then started dinner. I wasn't in the mood to make anything big. I grilled some chicken and steamed some brown rice. My dad would make a salad or something for him and mom when they got home to go with it. I was too tired to care.

Once I was done eating, I put away my dishes and decided to take a long hot bath to wash away all the day's crap. I drew up my bath, lit some candles, added bubbles, and started some light music. I climbed happily in, and as the room filled with steam, I was more relaxed almost instantly.

It was so sudden that I couldn't catch my breath. I was running through the woods being chased by a vampire, but it wasn't me. It was Adam, or I was Adam. It didn't matter what he did; he wasn't going to get away. He ran as fast as he could, looking over his shoulder. The vampire that I've seen a couple of times before in my visions was hanging back a little bit. It was like he was playing with Adam. I knew he could've caught Adam before Adam ever had the thought to run, but for whatever reason, he wasn't. I suppose the vampire finally got tired of playing with him because he pounced on Adam like a tiger stalking its prey. One second, Adam had the lead and was making some headway; the next, he was being thrown to the ground with so much force it knocked the breath out of me.

"You knew this was coming. Why bother running? You knew you were of no use to us without her," the vampire hissed in the evilest voice, a sound that made my blood run cold.

Why are they after Adam? Without who?

"I've been trying. She'll be mine again soon. You have to trust me. Where's the faith, man?" Adam asked as if they were best friends, and this was an everyday exchange. He didn't seem frightened in the least. *Is he really that stupid?*

"No worries, my friend. We will find another to replace you. With or without you, she will be ours."

In the blink of an eye, I could feel the vampire sink his razor-sharp teeth into the carotid artery in Adam's neck, slowly draining the life out of him. I could feel it like it was happening to me as the blood rushed out of my neck and into his mouth. I felt it all as I got sleepier and sleepier. Adam struggled at first, trying to force the vampire off him, but the fight was quickly drained out of him along with his blood.

I'm not sure how long this vision took, but when I came out of it, my bath water had gone cold, and tears were streaming down my face. It felt so real I instinctively reached for my neck. I just knew there were going to be bite marks and blood, but there was nothing. With shaky hands, I drained the bath and stepped out, quickly wrapping a towel around me. I walked down the stairs in a blur, not bothering to get dressed. I had to find my parents. Adam was going to die. I didn't have to look for long before I found them sitting at the kitchen table talking after dinner.

"Oh my god, honey, what's wrong?" My mom was at my side faster than my shocked brain could comprehend. I never saw her get up or move. As far as my mind was concerned, she magically appeared beside me, which was kinda creepy.

My tears started anew as I tried to tell them what happened. "Mom…Adam…Dad…visions," were all that came out between sobs.

"What? Honey, sit down," my dad told me as my mom led me to a chair.

I took a few deep breaths and tried to will my tears to stop at least enough for me to tell them what happened. "Oh god, Daddy, the visions. Adam…they're after Adam. Daddy, they're going to kill him. Daddy, you have to do something," I pleaded, collapsing into the chair and crying my eyes out again.

"Honey, who's after Adam? Why are they after Adam?" my dad asked in a panic.

"What? I don't know, Dad. They were talking about 'her.' 'You knew you were of no use to us without her.'"

"You and Adam broke up?"

"Yeah, Dad, but what does that matter? Are you even listening to me? A vampire is going to kill Adam! We have to do something!"

"Okay, sweetheart, it's okay. There's nothing to worry about. Why don't you just go upstairs to bed, and I'll call Adam's mom to check on him."

"Thanks, Daddy. Mom, will you come upstairs and lie down with me for a little bit?" I was still having issues getting my breathing under control, and as sad as it sounded, I needed my mommy. I felt like I was going to die if I was alone. I knew it was an irrational fear, but I couldn't shake it, not yet at least. The more visions I had, the more frightened I had become. Most of the time, it just takes some time to shake it off, but I've never known the person they were after.

"Sure thing, sweetie. Head on up and get dressed. I'll be there in a minute."

I just nodded as I headed up the stairs. I could hear my mom ask my dad, "What are we going to do?" But I never heard the reply. I cared. I wanted to listen to what they said, but I suppose my brain knew I couldn't handle anymore tonight because my feet never stopped until I was safe in my room. Upstairs in my room, I pulled on panties and threw on a T-shirt. I had just gotten into bed when my mom walked in. She climbed into bed behind me, shushing away the rest of my tears while rocking me and playing with my hair. My mom and I didn't always get along, but she was great at comforting me when I was sick or felt down, when I was scared or hurt. She was my mom, and in spite of everything, she always knew what to do to make things better. It wasn't long before I was fast asleep. Fortunately, it was actually a restful sleep. No doubt, thanks to my mom who was still asleep beside me when I woke up. It was like just by having her close, she was able to chase away all the bad dreams.

Careful not to wake her, I got out of bed and got ready for school. I pulled on a cut-off blue jean skirt, off the shoulder shirt, and a pair of boots. I drew my hair back into a tight bun and did my makeup. I grabbed my bag and was headed for my car when my dad touched my arm.

"Honey, we need to talk."

The look on his face told me everything. Adam was gone. With my breath held, I waited to see what he had to say. I had hope that it was something else.

"Adam's mom just called. She got the call early this morning. They found Adam's body in the woods. They said he had been hiking and got attacked by an animal," he explained, watching me carefully. I knew I was shaking my head way before my mouth caught up with my brain.

"What? No!" I protested, collapsing at the door and pushing my dad away from me. "You said it would be okay! You said you would take care of it!" I screamed at him. I knew I was going to hear this news sooner or later. I was just hoping for the latter. How could this happen?

My dad pulled me close despite my attempts to hurt him and keep him away, holding me as I started to hyperventilate. I felt the air slipping from my lungs as I tried so desperately to take it in. My eyelids became heavy as my heart pounded erratically in my ears. My chest began to burn; my lungs felt like they were on fire. I knew they were going to get him. I should have done something. I could've stopped this. Oh my god. I should've done something. No, he can't really be gone. This couldn't be happening. My mind was going a mile a minute, and despite my attempts, I couldn't get my breathing or brain under control.

I must have passed out; when I woke up, I was in my bed upstairs. I felt very odd as I struggled to open my weary eyes. My head was spinning, and my chest ached. My body felt like it had been hit by a truck. For all ten seconds, I forgot why I felt like this. But suddenly it all came rushing back, and I could feel my heart rate start to pick up again. I was already struggling for my next breath.

"Are you okay?" I heard him whisper from the corner of my room.

"Luke?" I cried as I tried sitting up to look at him. I needed him; I needed him to make it all go away.

"I'm here," he told me. He climbed into my bed, held me close, and rocked me.

With Luke there with me, I couldn't stop the tears as they started to fall, but thankfully I could breathe again. Luke was able to comfort me in a way no one else could. In his arms, I felt cherished and protected, loved and understood. In his arms, I felt at home, like everything my visions showed me was just a nightmare.

It felt as though I cried forever. Eventually, I must've cried myself back to sleep. I don't remember much from those first few days after Adam's death. I guess I was in shock. That's the only way that I could explain what was going on with me. I saw and heard everything that was happening around me, but it never really registered. I mean, I've seen some pretty messed-up things happen to people, thanks to my gift, granted I see it more as a curse. I guess the difference this time was it happened to someone I knew, someone I saw on a daily basis, someone I was close to. This time, I knew they were near, and I felt like they were waiting for me behind every door, in the shadows, and in my dreams.

I felt responsible; I should've been able to stop it. If I had, Adam would still be here, and I wouldn't be crying my eyes out, trying to find something in my never-ending closet that's black and appropriate to wear to a funeral. God, I hate this. I have nothing to wear. I sighed, finally giving up on my two-hour search. I had tons of things that were black, tons of things that I could wear to a funeral, but everything I pulled out didn't feel right. I'm sure it had to do with the fact that I didn't want to have to be doing this. *I'll just find something in the morning.*

I sighed, turning to stare at the disaster that was now my room and bed. It was too late to go shopping, and I didn't feel like shopping even if it wasn't. I didn't feel like doing anything. Throwing all my clothes off my bed and onto the floor, I crawled in. I was exhausted, but my brain and body wouldn't turn off. I lay there tossing and turning, with my mind screaming at me. *You could've stopped this. You should've stopped this. It's all your fault. You knew it was going to happen. It was your responsibility. Why didn't you stop it? You did nothing!* I hated it. Every night since Adam's death, it was the same. As soon as I would close my eyes, there was my inner voice waiting for me, screaming at me, and Adam's broken, lifeless body staring at me. I wish I knew how to shut her up, but eventually, she would quiet down or I would fall asleep anyways. I'm not sure which, not that it really mattered. Finally, I guess I fell asleep because before I knew it, I was waking up to what could've been a gorgeous day.

The day of Adam's funeral was the worst day of my life so far. I was up early. Granted I didn't sleep much since his death anyways, so I was pretty much up early or up late every day. I guess it really depends on how you want to look at it. If it weren't for what we had to do today, it would've actually been pretty. The sun was shining, and the birds were singing. It felt like Mother Nature was mocking me. If it weren't for the funeral today, I would've thought it was the perfect day, not too hot or cold, bright blue skies. Slowly I made my way out of bed and to the shower.

Once I managed to get myself bathed, I had the fun task of finally picking out the dreaded outfit. I needed something nice but not too nice and nothing I was over-the-top in love with because I knew after today I would never wear it again. With a sigh, I gave in and grabbed a knee-length black skirt, a black camisole, and a black three-quarter–length sleeve V-neck.

Once I was dressed, with my hair and makeup done, I headed downstairs to hopefully eat something. I didn't feel hungry, granted I never felt hungry anymore. To be honest, most of the time, I had an issue keeping food down at all. I missed Adam, as shocking as that was, and I missed Luke. Luke and his family finally went home last night, not that I was happy about it. One of them had been here at all times since Adam's death. Due to them not knowing Adam, they weren't going to attend the funeral today, so they decided to give us our space to mourn, like that was going to happen in twenty-four hours. No, I had a feeling this was going to be a pain and guilt I would feel for a very long time. I was sure they'll be back tonight, but for now, I was pretty much on my own. I mean, I had my parents, but it wasn't as though they gave me much comfort, not to say that anyone really did for that matter, but Luke made me feel safe. Thankfully, I would have Brooke once we got to the funeral, but I wasn't going to get to sit with her. Adam's mom wanted me to sit with her since I was his girlfriend. *God, this is going to be weird*, I thought, shaking my head. I didn't want to think. I just wanted to make it through today.

After looking around the kitchen for ten minutes, I finally gave up on food and grabbed a banana. At least I would have something in my stomach. I glanced at the clock on the wall as I walked past it on my way to the living room. We should be leaving in fifteen minutes. *Great, and the show begins.* I didn't want to do this. If there were any way I could've gotten out of it and not seem like a cold, heartless bitch, I would've. I felt guilty enough without hearing all the kind words everyone had to say about him. *Oh my god, what if they expected me to say something too? I can't. I just can't handle that,* I thought shaking my head.

Luckily for me, looking depressed worked for this because there was nothing I could do to change it. I had tried to cover some of the bags under my eyes this morning with makeup, but it didn't seem to do any good. Due to my lack of sleep without makeup, I looked like I had to black eyes with makeup...well, I still look like I have two black eyes, but at least they're less pronounced. *And this is why they tell you beauty sleep is important,* my inner voice snickered.

Before I knew it, my mom, dad, and I were in the car on our way to the funeral home. I wasn't even sure how I got into the car; at that point, I was just going through the motions. I was sitting in the back seat in a daze. I saw the scenery as we drove by, but I didn't see anything. It was all very strange to be in a daze—eyes unseeing, ears unhearing, there but not really there. Briefly I wondered if this is what it felt like to be a zombie, but it was just a fleeting thought.

When we pulled up outside the funeral home, the first thing that registered in my brain were Adam's parents. They looked broken; Adam's dad was basically holding his mom up. I knew I needed to go say something to them, but I had no clue what I was going to say. I was sixteen, I wasn't meant to handle things like this. How do you handle someone you were that close to dying? Once my dad had finally parked in the correct spot, it was time to get out. Apparently at a funeral, there is a right and a wrong way to do things, even something so simple as parking. As if everyone here didn't already have bigger things on their mind. I mean, we were at a freaking funeral, for goodness' sake; why does it matter where the hell we park? We were still in the car when I looked out the window and noticed all the cars around us were now hovering about two inches off the ground. I was in a bad mood and was going to have to figure out how to keep my anger in check if I didn't want to cause a scene. I hated the fact that my powers or gifts or whatever they were seemed to be tied to my emotions. Thankfully, it didn't appear as anyone noticed anything out of the ordinary…this time. I doubted I would be so lucky again.

As I got out of the car, I kept my eyes on the ground, waiting for my parents. I was going to need them if I was to make it through today. Thankfully, I guess they knew this because before my grief-riddled brain could process it, they were on either side of me, my dad with his arm around my shoulders and my mom holding my hand. Gradually, they led me toward Mr. and Mrs. Ross. My brain was screaming again, *Wrong way! Wrong way! Don't make me look these people in the eyes. Their son is dead because of me.* But evidently, my parents weren't tuned to my frequency because they just kept on going. The closer we got, the harder my heart pounded, the more difficult it became to breathe. My body felt like it was on fire; my mind was racing, and with every step closer, the more I struggled with each breath. *Please don't let me pass out. Please don't let me pass out*, was my mantra as we walked closer and closer to Mr. and Mrs. Ross. By the time we reached them, my mind was swimming in grief and paranoia. I just knew they were going to take one look at me and know Adam's death was entirely my fault. That's just what I needed for this day to turn into a witch hunt.

I think I heard my parents say that they were sorry for their loss, but I wasn't sure; I still hadn't found the courage to look up yet. Hesitantly, I lifted my head, making eye contact for the first time with Mrs. Ross, and that was it. The tears I had been trying to hold at bay all day came rushing forward.

"Oh, Rachel, sweetheart, come here," Mrs. Ross said, grabbing me and pulling me into a rib-breaking hug.

"I'm so sorry…I'm so so so sorry. I…I…I can't tell you how sorry I am," I whispered to her in between sobs, biting my tongue and holding back the thought that it was all my fault that was pushing to spills from my lips.

"Oh, sweetheart, I know, I know. It…it will get better," she whispered back, finally pulling away from me. Holding my hands and looking me in the eyes, she said, "You know, he loved you."

"I loved him too," I replied, breaking down again. What else could I say at that point? *Hey, your son used to be awesome, but in the end, he was borderline psychotic.* Somehow I didn't think that would've gone over too well, and I was always taught not to speak ill of the dead anyways.

"Thank you for coming," Mr. Ross said, barely giving me a glance.

I was never that close with Mr. Ross, but his cold behavior was odd. I'm sure it was simply due to his grief, and I didn't give it much thought. However, it was hard to see Mrs. Ross in this state. In many ways, I was closer to her than I was with my own mother. There were times I would go to their house just to hang out with her. We would go get our hair done, do mani-pedis, and go shopping.

"I think we better get her inside to sit down," my dad said, nodding to the Rosses as we walked past them. I was on autopilot just going where my parents steered me.

As my parents led me into the church, I glanced around, looking for my saving grace. I needed my best friend. Somehow, just her presence seemed to calm me, but I never saw her. Inside the church, we took a seat in the back and just sat there silently. I don't know, I guess maybe my parents were talking; but if they were, it all fell on deaf ears. Soon everyone started flowing into the church to take their seats, which meant my family and I were going to have to relocate. I wasn't looking forward to these seating arrangements.

My parents sat three rows behind me while I sat in the front row with Adam's family. I didn't belong up here. I needed my parents. I walked with his family to the casket, but I couldn't bring myself to look at his lifeless corpse. I had already seen plenty of it in my dreams. Quickly I followed his family, taking my seat next to his mother. I closed my eyes, doing my best to drown out the kind and loving words everyone had to say about him. I felt guilty, and I feared that it showed on my face. I wanted to feel sad or anything other than guilty. It didn't seem to matter how hard I tried; I couldn't drown it all out. When Adam's father took his position behind the podium to give his eulogy, I couldn't ignore the father's tears and broken voice.

"What can I say about my son…he was the joy of our lives. He meant the world to his mother and I. A cherished child taken too soon is something that I just can't understand. I spent the past few days staring at this piece of paper, trying to figure out what I was going to write. How do I explain my son's short life in a mere paper? How do I explain what he meant or who he was? I couldn't. I can't stand here and explain to all of you what he meant to his mother and I. I can't explain to you what he meant to you or others. I can't explain to you who he was or who he was going to be. If you are parents, then you already know what he meant to us. For those of you who are his peers, I imagine you all feel a loss as well, his teachers, family, and friends. All of you can feel a portion of the loss his mother and I feel. Only knowing him instantly changed anyone Adam met. Adam was an amazing son and friend. He was a great athlete and a kind soul. He was caring, loving, charismatic, and quite handsome, as I'm sure most of the young ladies here know." His dad chuckled; it was nice to see a small smile on his lips even as brief as it was. "He was my pride and joy. I can remember his mother and I talking about what he would be like when grown, his wedding and children, our grandchildren. These are all things that his mother and I will never know now. I can't help but think about all of the lost opportunities. How many missed hugs and taken-for-granted moments? How many times I wish I would've smiled and laughed instead of yelled. I know that Adam knew he was loved, but I sincerely doubt he had any idea how much he will be missed. Thank you all for coming." Slowly Mr. Ross made his descent back to the bench, grabbing Mrs. Ross and hugging her. It was becoming hard to breathe again; I could feel my skin getting itchy. I needed to get out of here.

I found a way to zone out for the rest, and soon we were all being directed out to our cars to follow the hearse to the graveside for yet more prayer. Prayer was supposed to bring us comfort, strength, hope, and peace. Today, however, it brought me none of these things. I did my best to drown it out and not allow my mind to wonder at the same time. *It's your fault. You could've stopped it*, my conscience started to scream again. That voice got louder and louder, and as it did, my anger grew stronger and stronger. I felt as though it was going to burst out of my chest. I was scared to open my eyes and see what I was doing when Brooke grabbed my hand. With Brooke by my side, I finally felt like I could breathe again. Unfortunately, the graveside service didn't take long, and before I really had time to catch my breath, it was over. A few amens, and we were in the car on our way to the Rosses for food and comfort, I suppose. I didn't fully understand going back to the loved ones' home after; to me, that didn't make any sense. It was like going, "Hey, I know your kid just died and all, but why don't you throw a party." It simply didn't make any sense, but who was I to argue with tradition.

At the Rosses, it appeared that the whole school showed up. I was getting quite a few nasty looks from girls whom I guess felt left out. I tried to stay out of the way. I wanted a corner to hide in, but unfortunately, I couldn't find one. So instead, I had to stand there and be repeatedly asked by strangers who I was and then be pulled into a tight hug. Always with the same line, "Oh, you poor dear." As far as I was concerned, we couldn't leave soon enough. Brooke drove herself to the funeral, so the lucky hag was able to go home right after. I thanked my lucky stars that my parents didn't want to stay long. It wasn't like they were close to Adam's parents or Adam for that matter, and I didn't know what to say or do, so I was happy to leave.

Once we made it back home, I went straight to my room. I had had my fill of people today and was looking forward to the solitude again.

I have few memories of the next few months; all I really remember was that it seemed like Luke never left my side. He stayed despite how many times I yelled at him, begged for him to just go away and leave me alone. I didn't want to die, but I was okay with no one ever seeing me again, which in my head at least, were two very different things. At that moment, I wanted nothing more than to disappear. I still felt that it was my fault Adam was dead, and the longer I felt like that, the more all the other deaths I've witnessed over the years felt like my fault too. I knew I needed to stop those feelings, but I didn't have even the foggiest idea how.

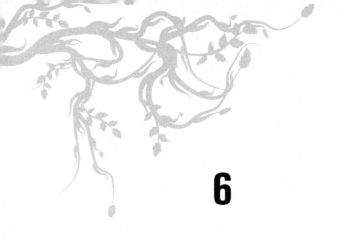

6

Seconds turned to minutes, minutes to hours, hours to days, days to weeks, and weeks to months. Yet the pain, fear, and paranoia stayed. I still felt as though something was out to get me. I'm not even sure why I was in so much pain. I tried to remind myself what a jerk Adam had become and how he had treated me, but my inner voice was always there reminding me that I saw it, I could've stopped it, it was my responsibility to have stopped it. Nothing seemed to help.

It didn't matter what he was like in those last few months. I knew somewhere inside him there had to have been the Adam I used to know and fell in love with. It was for that Adam that my heart mourned, I would remind myself. He had been a friend, and now he was gone. It didn't matter how he had treated me or what he had done. The last words we had said to one another were in anger. I would have given anything to take them back now.

The questions his death left me with didn't help either. Who was this "her" they were talking about? I had the sinking suspicion that my dad thought it was me, but why would these things want me? And if it were me that they were after, could all the other deaths and disappearances somehow be related to me?

I could feel myself growing stronger as I fought against the pain; I knew I had to break free of this haze I had been in. However, that was a lot easier said than done. I started to be able to breathe again; I guess that was a start. I pushed through trying to find my way out of the darkness. Surprisingly I spent more time in the solitude of my own mind praying, asking for guidance, strength, courage, and faith than I spent with friends and family. I needed help, and I was out of ideas on who to ask, so I turned to God. Perhaps he would have some grand advice that I had yet to see. I spent some time trying to analyze my feelings and my thoughts, catalog them, and understand them.

Luke had always been with me, but it hadn't seemed like he was there for me. No, it almost appeared like he was on guard duty, as if not to allow me to do anything stupid. Surely my parents knew me better than to think I might try to hurt myself.

I remember one night; I woke up to find that Luke wasn't there. I could hear talking downstairs, so I quietly tiptoed down to listen. I wasn't able to hear much. Everyone was there—Mark, Clair, Ryan, Luke, Nathan, my mom, and dad. I was listening, trying to make out what was being said when Nathan walked up behind me, touching my arm and scaring the crap out of me.

"Come on, Rachel, let's get you back upstairs. You don't need to hear any of this, sweetie," he spoke so sweetly. He helped me up the stairs and back to bed. I realized at this point everyone was treating me as though I was a mental patient. Who knows, maybe I should have been? I certainly didn't feel like myself. "Are you hungry? You've hardly eaten anything in days. I could make you something. Anything."

"No, thank you. I don't much feel like eating."

With a loud sigh and a nod of his head, he walked out of my room and back downstairs.

"Wait!" I shouted. "Please don't go. I…I don't want to be alone."

He was silent as he walked back into my room and laid down with me till I fell asleep, *I guess*, because when I awoke again, I was back in Luke's arms.

What I thought I had heard them say didn't make any sense to me. The more I thought about it, the more I was sure it had to have been a dream. I thought I had heard them talking something about evil and not allowing it to take me. I must be going crazy. Who would want a sixteen-year-old small-town girl? There was nothing special about me.

Nathan acted so mature, one would've never known that he was only fourteen years old. It really bothered me, knowing that I was in such a horrible state that a fourteen-year-old was taking care of me. Admittedly, what bothered me more was that it seemed everyone close to me was keeping a secret from me.

After that night, everything changed. Luke was always with me though I wasn't sure if it was because he wanted to be or if it was because he was scared to leave me alone. Despite the reason, I really did appreciate him being there. I didn't want to be alone; the idea of it frightened me. I couldn't explain it, but I had this fear of something being after me. I was literally petrified to be alone for any length of time, afraid that it was lurking behind doors and in the shadows, just waiting for its chance to get me. At times my fear was so bad that my mom would have to go with me to the bathroom because I was too scared to be alone. The things that had been so important before weren't anymore. I had been a straight As student; now I was barely getting by with Cs. I was head cheerleader and on the student body council, but I dropped it all; I couldn't see the point anymore. I didn't want to have to answer to anyone when I could barely hold on to myself.

School was horrible. Everyone wanted to know what happened to Adam, and since I was still known as his girlfriend, everyone came to me for answers. No one was happy about Luke and I being around each other. In the eyes of the school, I belonged to Adam. I felt as though I couldn't escape it. I would arrive at school with just enough time to make it to class and I'd leave as soon as the bell rang. But lunch was the worse. There was nothing I could do to escape the questions, the staring, and the whispers. Thankfully, I had Luke, Ryan, and Brooke. Every lunch period, they created what felt like a protective circle around me. They didn't stare or ask questions, and they never whispered. They didn't mind when I didn't talk, and no one ever mentioned it when the occasional tear slipped from my eyes. Wherever I was in my head, it was as though time held no place there.

I could recall everyone's excitement over Halloween. I could remember eating turkey and being with family. If I tried hard enough, I could briefly recall red, green, and snow. I knew it must've been Christmas, but I don't remember any of the enjoyment, happiness, and excitement that I always associate with Christmastime, that I associate with all the holidays.

Time continued as did life, and eventually I learned to move on, not to focus on what I couldn't understand. Before I knew it, it was time for the annual New Year's party that our town held every year. I'm not sure who convinced me to go, but I wasn't happy about it.

"But I don't want to go!" I cried when Luke and my parents had cornered me one afternoon after Christmas.

"I'm sorry, sweetie, but we aren't giving you a choice," my dad had said.

"Clair and I already bought you your dress. You're going to love it!" my mom tried to encourage.

"It will be good for you to get back into the swing of things," Luke stupidly piped in.

I glared at him. My parents forcing me was bad enough, but Luke too. *What a traitor.* I thought he was supposed to be on my side. "Fine," I reluctantly gave in, realizing that I couldn't win.

They didn't even give me time to try to get out of it. Those bullies waited until the night before to spring it on me. If I had more time, I would have faked illness, anything to have gotten me out of it.

The next morning, Clair came over early. She and my mom had plotted against me. Apparently, they had spent weeks planning this. The two of them had set up an at-home spa day for me. I woke up to the two of them bringing me my favorite breakfast in bed—cinnamon rolls and bacon. As soon as I finished, they rushed me off to a nice hot bubble bath they had drawn. Once I was relaxed and squeaky clean, they had me dress in a robe, sprayed some stuff in my hair and sat about doing my nails and toenails. Thankfully, after that, they allowed me a small reprieve for lunch, and then it was straight back to it. They spent the next three hours doing my hair and makeup. When they had finally deemed me ready, they helped me into my dress and ran off to get ready themselves.

I sat there in my room, staring at myself in the mirror. It was my reflection, but I hardly recognized the person staring back at me. I had changed so much. I had probably lost about ten pounds, which was a lot on my already petite frame. I was five feet four inches, and before all this, I had only weighed about 110 pounds. Now to be honest, I looked kinda sick.

"Honey, we're ready to go!" I heard my mom shout from downstairs.

You can do this, I reminded myself as I started my descent down the stairs. The dress Clair and my mom had gotten was gorgeous, a full skirt with a corset top. It was white satin with gold embellishments. They had gotten me matching gold-and-rhinestone stilettos. My hair was done up with the occasional strain down and curled; they had put glitter and rhinestones in my hair to really make it sparkle. My nails were white with gold tips. My mom had given me an amazing pearl and diamond gold choker; it had been my grandmother's, she told me. My dad had gotten me earrings, custom-made to match. I heard my father, Mark, and Luke gasp as I approached the bottom of the stairs. Luke was standing there like a real gentleman, holding out his hand to take mine.

"You look stunning," he told me.

"Thank you."

"I have something for you. The finishing touch," he explained, handing me a small square box. I studied it before opening it. For the first time in a long time, I felt that childhood excitement. I wanted nothing more than to shake the box and see what I could hear. I was really proud of myself that I managed to suppress that urge. Inside was a dainty pearl and diamond gold bracelet. It was fantastic, beautiful, and matched the rest perfectly.

"It was pretty in the box, but now it is breathtaking," he said while fastening it to my wrist. "I hope you like it."

"It's remarkable. I love it. Thank you."

No guy had ever given me a gift before—well, never a gift like this at least. Our parents had gotten a limo; I thought it to be a bit ostentatious, but I also thought everyone was trying to stun me out of the glumness. We had to stop on the way to pick up Ryan, Nathan, and their dates. I had been so consumed lately that I had no idea who either of them was taking. We picked up Nathan and his date, Michelle, first who lived right down the street; her family and mine had been friends for years. I knew her and her brother, Jeremy, quite well. As we pulled up to get Ryan and his date, I recognized the house. *Wow, when did that happen?* I thought to myself as Ryan and his date, my best friend, Brooke, got in.

"Holy crap. Rachel, you look amazing," Brooke said before she was even fully in the limo. She looked beautiful in a green full-length dress and her red flowing curls.

"Thanks, you too."

Brooke sat down right beside me, and once everyone was involved in their own conversations, I leaned into her. "So… Ryan, huh?"

She smiled at me; I could see her blush even in the dim lights of the limo. "God, Rachel, he's gorgeous and sweet and gorgeous and fun, and I don't know, we just started hanging out, and well…"

I couldn't help laughing. "I'm happy for you."

Apparently my laughter alerted others to our conversation because Ryan quickly asked, "Talking about me?"

"You wish," I told him with one of my first real smiles in a long time. I had forgotten how much I missed the stupid banter Ryan and I shared.

The party was held at the town hall, a historic building in the center of town. I knew everyone there practically. *Ah, the joys of a small town.* Most of us were born and raised here. We entered the ballroom, and I could feel the eyes of everyone around me, watching me, examining me, checking to see if they could tell exactly when I would crack. *Not long, if everyone keeps staring.*

"They're staring," I whispered to Luke as he led me to the dance floor after we had discarded our coats.

"No, angel, they are admiring."

"Hmm… Well, admiring still looks and feels a lot like staring."

He spun me as the music started to play, ignoring my complaints. I had been attending the town dances since before I could walk. Over the years, I had managed to become quite the good little dancer; I was shocked to see how well he danced though. We floated around the dance floor, spinning and twirling to the music. It was like straight out of a Disney movie. It was perfect. As the song ended, they announced that it was time for the annual father-daughter dance. Luke kindly handed me off to my dad.

"You look amazing" he complimented, spinning me into a small dip.

"Thank you, Daddy."

"I'm so glad to see you smiling and enjoying yourself again, sweetheart. It's been too long."

"Me too, Daddy. It's nice to start to feel a little bit more like myself again," I said, giving him a tighter squeeze. As soon as our song came to an end, there was a young man I had never seen before waiting for a dance with me.

"Do you mind, sir?" he asked my father.

"No, not at all. She's all yours," my father said, giving me a kiss on the cheek and handing me off to this stranger. The young man, with one hand firmly around my waist and the other hand in mine, pulled me in close and started to twirl us around the dance floor as the next song began to play. If I was to be honest, he was shockingly good-looking, even compared to Luke.

"I'm sorry. I don't mean to be rude, but do I know you?" I asked after a moment.

"I don't know, Rachel. Do you know me?" I was thrown off by his response. What kind of answer was that? I tried to pull back, but his grip around my waist tightened. "Ah ah ah...your daddy and boyfriend are watching, and I must say Luke doesn't look too pleased. I guess he doesn't like to share. Too bad you would make a lovely trophy. Now stop fighting and play nice, would you? I'm not here to hurt you, and if I were, you'd already be dead."

"Well, thanks, that's just so comforting. What is it that you do want then?"

"I'm here to help you, Rachel. My name is Dustin, and my being here is my death warrant, but I saw no other way. I had to warn you. The end is coming, and you must be ready."

"What do you mean being here is your death warrant?"

"I'm a vampire, Rachel, and being here puts me on the wrong side of things. Look, just understand that I will help where I can. Also, you should know, not all that you hold close are who you think they are."

The song ended, and he was gone. I stood there for a moment in a daze, trying to figure out exactly what had just happened. What did he mean not all were who I thought they were? What kind of cryptic crap is this?

"Who was that?" Luke asked, coming up behind me and startling me out of my head.

"I have no idea," I told him truthfully.

"What did he want?"

I quickly weighed my options and decided telling Luke the truth probably wasn't the best of ideas. "Just a dance," I told him instead.

"A dance? Really? You didn't look too happy. Did he say something that upset you?"

I sighed, looking into his eyes. Luke was always my defender.

"I don't know what he wanted," I said again, a bit firmer this time. I knew I could tell Luke anything and everything, but there was this feeling in my gut telling me that I needed to keep what Dustin said to myself.

"I know you aren't telling me something, but fine, I will let you keep your secrets for now," Luke joked, wiggling his eyebrows at me and spinning me back onto the floor for the next song.

The remainder of the night was normal. I didn't mention Dustin or his warning to anyone. I was starting to have fun, and the last thing I needed was for my family to have a meltdown. *Oh, hey, so you all wanted me to come to this dance. I had a lot of fun. Oh, and did I mention I danced with a vampire that gave me a grave warning about the end coming?* Yup, that was a surefire way to have everyone in a panic and making a scene.

We all danced the rest of the night away. I actually found myself laughing and smiling to my surprise; it felt good. I was lost in the magic of it all, taken by complete surprise when they announced that it was time to start the countdown.

"Ten…nine…eight…seven…six…five…four…three…two…one!" everyone chanted. "Happy New Year!"

Luke spun me into his arms as he dipped me with a passionate kiss; it was incredible. Then we all continued dancing into the wee hours of the morning.

7

After that night, things started to look up. Life was getting better, easier. Dare I say it, life was almost good again. A week later was my seventeenth birthday, and it seemed that was all my family wanted to talk about anymore. Mom and Clair spent what I now realized had to have been at least weeks' planning.

The day of my birthday dawned with yet another breakfast in bed. This time it was Greek yogurt and fresh fruit, another of my favorites, and my parents sang me "Happy Birthday." Unfortunately, after a long breakfast with them, I was now running late for school.

I quickly got dressed and ran to my car. I made it just in time to hear the last bell ring. I ran to my locker, praying when I got to Ms. Brady's class I wouldn't be in too much trouble. To my surprise, there were balloons all over my locker, and my friends were waiting beside it with cupcakes. Apparently we were playing hooky from our first period today; I suppose I could live with that. Outside in the quad, they sang me "Happy Birthday," and we sat out there, eating cupcakes and laughing and joking. It felt marvelous; it was as if no time had passed. However, much too soon, the bell was ringing, and it was time to get back to reality. I was sad to have to leave, but it was a blast while it lasted. I couldn't go anywhere in the school today without people greeting me. It was actually a huge surprise that several of my teachers gave me the day off, and a lot of people gave me flowers.

I wondered how much of this my mom had arranged, granted I couldn't quite figure out how she could've done it. When the school day was finally over, I was looking forward to the weekend. I had gotten so many flowers and balloons at school that Luke had to help me carry all of them to my car.

When I got home was another story entirely. My mom must've spent all day decorating; the whole house was done in lime green and bright pink, my favorite colors. There were candles, flowers, candy, cookies, cake, and presents everywhere. By the looks of things, she had to be throwing me a party that I knew nothing about.

My mom came out of the kitchen. "Oh, honey, you're finally home. Good! Go upstairs and start getting ready. Your dress is already up in your room. Oh, and here, give me those. I'll put them in water for you," she said, taking all the flowers in my hand.

I stood there for a moment in a daze, and my mom started pushing me toward the stairs. Thankfully I took the hint and started walking. *She's a pushy little bugger today*, I thought.

In my room, I deposited my things on the floor and went in search of this dress my mom was talking about. I found it hanging on the hook on the inside of my closet door. It was breathtaking—bright-pink strapless dress about knee length with a lime-green sash under the bust. She had even gotten me lime-green shoes to match. I quickly jumped into the shower and started getting ready; I couldn't wait to put on my new dress.

Two hours later, I was finally prepared to make my grand entrance yet again. Once downstairs, I was shocked to see everyone. It appeared that mom and Clair had invited the whole town. The night was perfect. I tried my best to make my way around the rooms and talk to everyone, but I'm sure I missed a few.

Mom and Clair had hired a catering company, and there were waiters walking around with trays of all of my favorite foods. Around ten, my dad called it was time to open my presents. I didn't think I had ever received so many gifts in my life. I got tons of clothes, shoes, jewelry, books, movies, music, and cash. I have to say it was probably the best birthday party I have ever had, but by midnight I was exhausted. I blew out my candles, and luckily, the party ended soon after.

Saturday after the party, I slept in until noon, and then it was back to reality. It didn't take long for my mind to start to wander again. There was still so much about Luke and his family that I just didn't understand, but I was trying not to let it get to me. I remember I once had attempted to ask my dad about Luke and his family.

"Rach, they're just like us," he explained. "A loving and caring family."

Just like us, the words echoed in my head now.

What did he mean "just like us"? I knew that we weren't exactly what you would call normal; at least not what I felt was normal. We were different from any other family I had met living in our small town. Different than most families living anywhere I imagined. I couldn't understand what he meant by "they were just like us." It's hard for me to wrap my head around my family's weirdness, but then to imagine another family out there that could do the kinds of things we could. It gave me a headache. Could it be possible? I didn't see how.

Take my dad, for instance. He could will things to happen the way he wanted. All he had to do was think about a problem and the outcome he wanted. Then it would happen just the way he imagined it. Man, I could picture how easy school would be.

Then there were my visions. I hated them and never felt they were really a power. I mean, come on, my dad could will things to happen, and I knew before people died or got abducted or whatever. It's so not fair. Granted, I could move objects with my mind, but that was just more trouble than it was worth. That's all I need to be known as the next Carrie.

"Being able to see the future is no small thing, sweetie," my dad would remind me.

Well, it wasn't like I could see the future—just when someone was going to die, be kidnaped, or tortured. It wasn't an exact science. I very rarely got to see any of the good things—a wedding, a graduation, a first kiss. I would have a vision, but they felt more like a dream type thing about people I didn't know and had never seen before. When I came back, I knew that they were going to die or whatever. I knew how, and I knew it was inevitable, but I didn't know when exactly. Not very good considering everyone is going to die sooner or later. Granted I normally had some idea where, but can you imagine how much it must suck to die, how painful it must be? I can because every time I have a vision, I live through it with them. I'm seventeen, and if I remember correctly, I have died 342 times since I started having my visions.

"You have a very special gift," my dad would try to assure me. "When you learn to control it, you'll be able to see many things past death and destruction." *Learn to control it.* Yeah, that was easy for him to say. I didn't know how or why I knew the things I knew. I just knew them.

Is this the kind of different my dad had meant? If this was the case, Luke already knew everything, or so it seemed, so why wouldn't he just tell me? Why hide it? With that, a light bulb turned on. *Wow…no…it couldn't be…could it?* When I was younger, every night, as my dad tucked me into bed, he would tell me a fairy tale, or at least that's what I thought it was, until now. It made perfect sense why the Rockwells came here, how my dad and Mark know each other, why these horrible things are happening.

"Long, long ago in a faraway place, there lived the guardians. In the beginning, there were hundreds. Now there are two. What came to pass left the world in a pit of despair," began the fairytale. "They were the guardians of the earth, sent here by a higher power to protect the people of the land from the supernatural wonders that sought out to harm them. The guardians had unimaginable powers. Some could control the earth. Others, air. Some could control the water, and more could control fire."

"Among them, there was one, Madeline, the smallest but sweetest. She held the gift of foresight. She could see the future for all its pain and glory. The guardians came to her for guidance, for understanding, and for the knowledge of the future. They would seek out the supernatural ones who sought out evil and destroy them before they could harm or be discovered. This gift, though great, came at a high cost. You see, it took a lot of both mental and emotional strength to see the future. It left her drained and unable to defend herself. Her protection was one of the guardians' highest concerns. It was their sworn duty. They knew without Madeline, the balance in power would shift, throwing the world into darkness."

"They were all great warriors, sent to fight a never-ending battle. It was the darkest of their days when the other guardians discovered that Madeline had been taken. Evil used her gifts against the guardians. One by one, the guardians were killed until only two remained. These two, fueled by their anger, left their homes to seek out a new future, to rebuild what they had lost. They took it upon themselves to create a new kind of guardian, ones that couldn't be as easily tracked by evil. They both soon settled down and married, having children. The older had three boys. Though each of his children was amazing and had great gifts, none of them held the gift of foresight. The younger was blessed with only one child, a beautiful baby girl. This little girl, from the moment, she was conceived, held the gift of foresight so strong that while her mother carried her, she could see the child's visions of the future."

Always, my fairytale held the same tragic story and the same abrupt ending. I would pester my dad, "What, Daddy? What happens next?"

"I don't know, my dear sweet Rachel. Perhaps when you are grown and have children of your own, you will know the ending and be able to pass it along to your own children," he told me.

Was it possible? Could what I thought was a mere fairy tale actually be the story of my ancestry? The doorbell interrupted my thoughts.

"Just a sec!" I shouted, coming down the stairs. I opened the door to see Luke. I couldn't stop myself; I hit him as hard as I could in the chest.

"Ow! What the hell was that for?" he asked, rubbing his chest.

"Really? You've known this whole time? I've basically been going nuts trying to figure it all out, and never once, even for a moment, did you stop and think. Hmm, maybe I should tell her? God, you're an ass."

"I see…so I take it you finally put all the pieces together."

"No, I'm just a raging lunatic. Yes, Luke, I figured it all out and no thanks to you."

"Rachel, our parents wouldn't let us tell you."

"No, stop right there. If you had cared about me, it wouldn't have mattered what our parents said. You would've told me."

"Damn it. That's not fair, and you know it."

"I don't know what I know anymore. What I thought was a damn fairytale I'm now thinking is an actual story, and do you even realize how crazy that is? How crazy all of this is?"

"Rachel, I'm sorry. But listen to what you just said. Even if I would've tried to tell you, do you really think you would've believed me?"

"Of course I would've. It's you."

"Wow…really? You are such a damn liar, and you know it."

"Well, that's not really the point now, is it? You should've told me."

"And like I said, I'm sorry! Look, why don't we go for a small hike, and we can talk, okay?"

I nodded my head and followed him toward the hiking trail that was off the side of our land. I was so mad at him, at all of them. I mean, why in the hell wouldn't anyone tell me. How could one keep something like that from his child? My dad knew all along what my visions were and what they meant, yet he said nothing. How was I supposed to protect myself when I didn't even know I was in danger? Although I guess I kinda always knew I was in danger. I mean, that's why my visions frighten me so much because I always think they're after me.

"I grew up my whole life knowing all this. What would you have honestly said to me if I just told you you were a magical thing born to save the earth?"

"I would've thought you were a mental patient who escaped and is here to kill us all," I joked halfheartedly. "So what do we do now? Oh…oh does this mean I get to learn how to use weapons or something cool like that?" I had finally found an upside to all this.

"No. One of the reasons my family and I moved here was to help protect you. Your father knew that your powers were getting stronger, which means it's easier for them to find you. We are supposed to be your weapon."

"Wait…really? No one tells me I'm a superfreak, and now I'm not even allowed to learn how to protect myself, and let's not mention the fact that my boyfriend is basically my supernatural bodyguard! Oh my god. Please tell me that's not the reason you're with me—"

"Wow, do you really think so little of me? Because that hurts."

"I don't know what I think of you right now. So tell me then, Luke, why are you with me?"

"No, I'm not going to do this with you. I love you, and you know that."

My face lit on fire, and I think my heart stopped. He did not just tell me he loves me for the first time in the middle of a fight. He loves me? Wow, I think I might need to sit down for the rest of this fight.

"What did you just say?" Hey, a girl has to be sure, right? Okay, maybe I just wanted to hear it again.

"What? I said…" I could see the realization dawn on him as he walked over and cradled me in his arms. "I told you I love you."

The grin on my face felt like it was going to split my cheeks open. "I love you too…but I'm still mad at you."

"Of course you are," he said, shaking his head, and gave me a quick kiss. We continued walking, happier now.

"Luke?"

"Yeah?"

"What did you mean when you said now that my powers are getting stronger, they can find me?"

Luke stopped to look at me and took a deep breath before starting to walk again. "Rachel, they can sense us due to our powers, and in some ways, we can sense them. Granted, it's easier with vampires. The older they are, the easier they are to sense, but the same kinda thing goes for us. The stronger we are, the easier it is for them to sense us. Once they sense you if you are strong enough, they will hunt you to the ends of the earth if they have to."

"Why?" I asked. Afraid I didn't want to know the answer.

"Look…, it doesn't matter. We are all here to protect you, and I would never let those things touch you."

"They would kill them then," I guessed. Not that I was really thinking about any of that anymore. I still hadn't told Luke or my dad about the vampire on New Year's, and I have to admit, at the moment, I felt awful about that. "Luke…I have to tell you something."

We were just about to the top of the small mountainside that my house was built near when Luke grabbed my arm, covered my mouth, and pulled me off the trail into the brush. He whispered quietly in my ear, "It's fine. I heard footsteps, and I just want to find out who's been following us. Granted, I'm pretty sure I already know. I'm going to let you go. Just be quiet. Okay?"

I nodded as he let go of me. We didn't have to wait very long before we could hear male voices in the distance. I was shocked and a little scared; I knew no one should be on this trail. The only way to get to it was from the back of my house. As the voices got closer, Luke looked at me, rolled his eyes, and put his finger to his lips. The voices got closer and closer until finally we could see them. Luke held up his fingers, one, two, three! He grabbed my hand, and we jumped out at them.

The looks on their faces were to die for, pale with the look of terror in their eyes; they were so scared. Luke and I instantly started laughing.

"Come on, guys, it's not funny. You two scared the crap out of me! I thought you were wolves or something," Nathan whined.

Ryan came over without a word and punched Luke as hard as he could right in the shoulder. Poor Luke, he was getting hit by everyone today. Then he turned toward me.

"No! No! Ryan! *Stop!*" I begged with my hands out in front of me, still laughing, "Ryan, no!"

He picked me up and tossed me over his shoulder. "I bet you thought that was pretty funny, huh, Luke?" Ryan asked with a devilish look in his eyes "Well…I bet you can't find us!" He taunted as he took off running into the forest with me still over his shoulder. He ran faster than any normal human could. It was insane.

I was a little scared, even though I knew Ryan would never hurt me or let anything happen to me. It was still terrifying, having just figured all this out and not knowing what any of them could do. He stopped when we got to this enormous old oak tree. He glanced up at one of the big branches way above us. It had to be at least forty feet above our heads.

"You might want to hold on tight," he informed me while shifting to cradle me in his arms. Unaware of what stupid thing he was about to attempt, I quickly settled into his arms and held on like my life depended on it, for all I knew, it very well might. He took a deep breath, knelt down, and sprang up. In one swift movement, he had propelled our bodies to the branch that had been way above our heads a moment ago.

"Holy cow, Ryan! How did you do that?" I exclaimed. "Never mind." I shook my head, while he laughed at me. A few moments later, I heard a brief sound of leaves rustling. The next thing I knew, Luke had me in his arms.

"Found you!" Luke whispered in my ear and gave me a kiss. It sent shivers down my whole body.

"I knew you would. But can you get me down from here…please?" I begged. I wasn't afraid of heights, but I wasn't climbing any trees either.

"Sure, close your eyes." And with that, he stepped off the side of the branch we were on. I gripped his neck as tight as I could and screamed. We were safely on the ground in an instant.

"Rachel, you can let go now. Sweetie, we're fine, we're on the ground."

I shook my head and scrunched my eyes tighter shut and held on for dear life. I had a feeling I was going to be afraid of heights for a while now. *Great. Thanks, boys*, I thought sarcastically. The boys laughed at me pretty hard as Luke fought to free himself from my tightening clutch. Once I had my feet firmly back on the ground, I finally started to calm down.

"Okay, newbie here, guys." I gestured at myself. "Take it a little slower, will ya?"

This made them roar with laughter again. When Luke was able to find his composure, he said, "Sorry, sweetie, we didn't intend to frighten you, but you know that you were never in any real danger. Don't you?"

"I know. Okay, so now that I am aware of everything, what's everyone's superpower?" I asked once I got my heartbeat back under control. I couldn't wait to find out. I wished I had real powers.

"I can control storms," Nathan said happily. Finally, he sounded like the kid he was as he made it start raining. "I can cause a storm of biblical proportions if I want to." He shrugged.

"I can control fire," Luke said after Nathan had stopped the rain. "Granted, it's not that cool unless you've already got some fire to work with." He pulled out a lighter and set his hands on fire. I watched in amazement as they turned into big flaming balls of fire. Luke wound up like he was going to pitch a baseball and threw the fire at a tree. Transfixed, I saw the tree go up in flames. Evidently his fire worked much faster than ordinary fire because the tree was ash in seconds. Nathan conjured rain to put out the little embers of fire that remained.

"I can control the earth," Ryan said.

"Aren't you going to show me?" I asked.

"God, this isn't show-and-tell, Rachel," Ryan snapped. It was very odd and not like Ryan at all, but what was I supposed to do?

"Um, okay, you're right. Sorry. Well, all of your powers are really cool. What about your dad?" I asked, trying to change the subject and hide my anger from being snapped at for no apparent reason. *What's with Ryan?* I wondered.

"Well, our dad can teleport. All he has to do is concentrate on a place, and he will be there. He has also learned over the years if he concentrates on one of us, he can teleport to wherever we are as well. Nathan used to get lost a lot when he was younger," Luke informed me. Nathan turned beet red and put his head down.

"Hey, don't blame it only on me. I guess you don't remember sinking off with Lauren and dad having to find you," Nathan taunted back.

"Who's Lauren?" I asked as Luke stared daggers at his brother.

"No one," Luke snapped.

Nathan laughed, only upsetting Luke more. "Lauren is his ex-girlfriend."

Hmm. Ex-girlfriend. Sneaking off. Maybe my Luke wasn't as innocent as he liked to appear.

"Wow, those are all really cool. Mine and my dad's kinda suck by comparison," I said getting us back on subject despite the sudden surge of jealousy that now rushed through my veins.

"Rachel, yours is the most important. Without yours, ours are pointless," Nathan said, giving me a hug. That boy was too sweet for his own good. One of these days, he'd get his heart broken. I just hope he could come out of it being the same sweet and kind person he was now.

"I know. That's what everyone keeps telling me, but it doesn't make it cool or fun like the rest of yours, but thank you," I said, hugging him back. We all started walking back to my house as the sun set.

"Hey, Rachel, what did you want to tell me earlier?" Luke asked on our way back.

"Huh? When?"

"Before my brothers showed up, you said you wanted to tell me something."

"Oh right," I said, remembering. I really didn't want to tell him, but I kinda felt like I had to. "The guy at the New Year's dance...do you remember him?" I asked, hesitating, knowing that if I said something, there was no going back, but I still wasn't sure I wanted to tell them.

"Yeah."

"His name was Dustin."

"You're kinda driving me crazy here. Just spit it out."

"He said he was a vampire, and he wanted to warn me the end was coming and that not everyone was who they said they were."

"A vampire! And you're just telling me about this now, why?" Luke yelled.

"Rachel, this is serious. If they already know how to get to you, you could be in a lot more danger than we realized," Ryan told me.

"We need to tell our parents," Nathan whispered.

"Look, my parents will be home tonight, and I'll tell them, I promise."

My parents were due to be back late that evening, so as soon as we got back, all the boys left. I didn't want Luke to go, but it was better than my dad coming home and finding him here. Not that any of them really wanted to leave after what I had just told them, but I reassured them that I'd be fine, and they were only a phone call away. Where my parents knew Luke stayed the night all the time when they were home, it was entirely different when they were gone. Once I said good-bye to the boys, I headed inside to make myself some dinner.

8

I rummaged in the fridge and pantry forever until settling for mac and cheese. I started making it and decided to go turn on the TV while it cooked. I hated the silence; it always managed to creep me out. In the silence, I always heard things that weren't there, a knock or whisper—they were normal things, but when alone at night and with an imagination like mine, they were terrifying. That's when I heard it—a sound like a wolf howling out in pain.

That's odd, I thought to myself. I noticed that it sounded as though it was moving closer to the house. Granted there were wolves in the woods behind my house, but it was still unusual to hear them this close and even stranger for them to sound like they were moving closer. I blew it off as my imagination getting the best of me again and went to finish making my dinner.

On my way back to the kitchen, I noticed that the front door was standing wide open. *Hmm*, I thought. *I had shut that. Oh well.* I went and shut the door, making sure I locked it this time. I was a little creeped out, but I kept reminding myself of all the logical explanations. *The wolf is just an animal, and the trees can make things sound different than they are. I must have forgotten to shut the door all the way, and the wind blew it open. See, Rachel, perfectly normal*, I reminded myself again and again.

I was just about to sit down to eat when I heard the doorbell. It startled me, causing me to knock over the chair I was about to sit in. *Who could be ringing my doorbell this late?* I wondered. It was 9:30 at night, I confirmed glancing at my watch. Sighing, I grabbed the phone on my way to the door, just in case I needed it to call the police. Carefully I glanced out the window to see who was at the door before opening it. *Couldn't be too safe.* I guess I thought I would recognize an axe murder.

"Brooke? Oh my god, what are you doing here? Are you okay?" I asked, opening the door and noticing her bloodshot eyes and dirty torn clothes.

"I needed some help and didn't know where else to go."

"Oh, sure. Come in please," I said, shocked at the sight of my best friend like this. ", what happened?"

"I was running in the woods and fell down."

"Really? You fell down?" I questioned in a disbelieving voice. "Why were you in the woods at this time to begin with? You know how dangerous that can be." I felt like a parent scolding a child.

"Do you think I could borrow some clothes and take a quick shower?" she asked, clearly avoiding my questions.

"Umm, sure. You know where it all is."

"Yeah, thanks, Rach."

"Hey, do you want me to call someone to pick you up?"

"No! No, it's fine," she said, heading for the shower.

"Well then, you're staying here," I yelled up after her.

I went back to the kitchen to finish eating. When I heard the shower start, I quickly grabbed the phone and called Luke. Something just didn't add up. I couldn't explain it, but all of my senses told me something was off, way off.

"Miss me already?" he answered.

"Hey…umm, can you come over?"

"Are you okay?" he asked, panicked. I guess I sounded more shaken than I realized.

"I'm fine. I just need you to come over, and can you bring Ryan with you, please?" I told him. "Oh, and don't tell anyone that the two of you are coming here. Okay? And, Luke, hurry." I'm not sure if it was the night or what, but I was letting myself get completely freaked out. Luke and Ryan couldn't get here soon enough.

"Be there in five."

Five? The boy's crazy, I thought. He lived at least fifteen minutes away; even if he sped up, there was no way he'd make it here in five. I finished my dinner, put the leftovers away, and did my best to keep my fear under control. I had just started doing the dishes when I heard a faint knock at the door.

"My god, Luke! How fast were you driving?" I asked as I opened the door.

"What's going on?"

"When the three of you left earlier, I came inside to make me dinner. Then I heard what sounded like a wolf howling, but it sounded like it was getting closer, which is weird. Anyhow I noticed the front door was standing wide open, and I could've sworn I shut it when I came in, so I closed and locked it. Then Brooke came. Her eyes were bloodshot like she had been crying. Her clothes were dirty and torn."

They looked at one another, stunned.

"She asked to borrow some clothes. She's upstairs in the shower now."

"Are you sure?" Luke asked.

"Am I sure? No, I imagined the whole thing! God, Luke, I think I know what my best friend looks like."

"No, that's not what I meant. It's just that Brooke had been at our house with Ryan. She left after you called, so we could come over here."

Panic covered my face as real fear set in. "Then who's upstairs in my shower?"

"I don't know, but I'm sure as hell going to find out," Ryan told me, heading toward the staircase. "Just stay here."

"What?" I asked in panic. "You're not going to leave me down here alone!" I protested.

"Just stay behind us," Luke said.

I nodded and turned toward the opposite direction, heading for Daddy's study.

"Where are you going?" they asked chasing after me.

"Look, I may not have superhuman strength or speed or grace for that matter. But what I do have is brains," I told them while grabbing the key off Daddy's desk and unlocking the safe. I opened it and moved out of the way. They looked at the safe, then at me in disbelief. "Take what you want. Just please try not to damage the house too much. My mom would freak out, and for the love of God, try not to shoot each other or yourselves. Please."

I had always wondered why Daddy had so many different types of weapons. I just never got a real answer, but I was grateful now. Somewhere in the back of my mind, I just thought he was one of those crazy gun guys. Who would ever need silver or wood bullets? Granted, it all made perfect sense now.

Ryan grabbed a snub-nosed .38 and a few extra rounds, and Luke grabbed 1911 pistol and some extra magazines. I thought their choices in weapons were strange. I knew the guns they were grabbing but only because I had grown up with my dad teaching me about his weapons. Ryan's choice was a short barrel revolver whereas Luke's was a full-sized semiautomatic .45 caliber pistol. I would've just gone with a shotgun, but I suppose they knew what they were doing. After all, they had been trained for this kind of stuff their whole lives.

We were headed up the stairs when I realized that the shower was no longer running. It caused my panic to slightly rise as we made our way to the bathroom first—it was clear—then to my bedroom, which was dark except for my closet light.

You go left. I'll go right. Rachel, you stay here, Luke motioned to us. I felt like I was in some awesome action movie except I realized there was a very real chance one of us could die or be seriously hurt. I stayed right at the door while they sneaked their way toward my closet. *One, two*, Luke held up his fingers.

I was watching with anticipation when I noticed a shadow out of the corner of my eye coming from down the hall. I quickly tiptoed to go investigate when out of nowhere, two big furry arms grabbed me, one arm around my waist and the other over my mouth. In a panic, I shoved my elbow into its gut with as much force as I had, at the same time biting down on one of the fingers that covered my mouth. I've always heard that when in a life-or-death situation, things happen in slow motion; I don't know if that's true or not, but it wasn't working for me. Instead, I felt like I was working on pure adrenaline. I didn't really have thoughts at the moment; it was instinct, I guess. The monster let go, and I screamed for Luke as I took off running down the hall. I didn't get very far before whatever it was that looked like Brooke was standing in front of me. She had stepped out of one of the spare rooms directly into the path between Luke and me. Forcing me to stop and look for a place to hide when the furry thing grabbed me again.

"No!" I pleaded, struggling to get away.

Luke and Ryan had just made it into the hall. Everyone stood still for what felt like forever. I didn't know if it was shock or fear, but I watched in slow motion as Ryan raised the snub-nose and took a shot at the Brooke look-alike. Finally, the slow motion. *Yay.* Unfortunately, she was standing right in front of me; and when he took the shot, she jumped out of the way leaving me to get nicked in the shoulder. I knew I would live, but it still hurt like hell. I take it back. *I don't like slow motion anymore.*

"Holy shit, Ryan! Stop! You hit Rachel, you idiot!" Luke yelled, shoving his brother as he got ready to try and take another shot. Luke looked up and deep into my eyes, he asked, "Are you okay?" When I nodded (I didn't trust my voice), Luke sighed, shaking his head. I could see the struggle he was having in his eyes. Did he let them take me or fight and risk me getting hurt further? When he looked up, I could see that he had made his decision. "Do you remember today in the woods? Don't be scared. It will all be okay. I will find you, Rachel. I will always find you," he encouraged.

"Luke!" I screamed as the monsters took me out the window.

Fear set in quickly, and I must have passed out, granted I guess it could've been from the pain as well. When I awoke, I didn't know where I was. The room was pitch-black; the walls and ground were cold and damp, like stone. I tried to calm myself down, but it was hard when I couldn't even see my hand in front of my face. I knew I needed to listen for any sounds that may give me a clue as to where I was. Or at least I knew that's what they always did in the movies. Hopefully then I might be able to find a way to get out of this hellhole those things had dragged me into.

I could hear faint voices. *The monsters that brought me here*, I thought. I could hear some type of running water. *Hmm. Stone. Cold. Water*. We must be in some type of cave or tavern, not at all unlikely with all the mountains. *God, I hope I'm right, and we aren't in a sewer or something*, I thought. I could still hear the voices, but they were getting closer now. *Well, this is it*. My mind went into overdrive. *I'm going to die, and the world will cease to exist*. Wow, really? That was a little melodramatic even for me. Oh well, in fifteen years, when I tell this story to my kids, I'll just leave that part out, assuming I live for another fifteen minutes, let alone fifteen years.

Just then, a boulder moved, and I could see a dim light. It took my eyes a few seconds to adjust even to the dim light after being in the dark for so long. When they finally did, I could see the furry beast; he had a woman with him. He threw her into the prison with me, set a lantern down just inside the opening, and slowly backed out. I watched as he blocked any hope of escape I had with a huge boulder. *The woman—who is she?* I wondered. She was older than me, but not old—probably close to my mom and dad's age. I looked at her curiously as she slowly walked toward me. She seemed to know her way around and definitely wasn't as afraid as I was as she casually took a seat on the floor.

"Hello, Rachel. I am very sorry about all this. I wish there were another way," she said to me with pain etched on her face. *Another way for what? Why was she in so much pain? How did she know my name? What was going on?*

"Who are you?" I tried to ask, but my voice broke, giving away how frightened I truly was.

"I'm Madeline."

The guardian from my fairy tale. I had so many questions to ask, but I couldn't manage to speak. I just sat there thinking and looking like an idiot. *What is she doing here? How did they find me? What are they going to do with me? Will I ever see my parents again?* With that thought, I started to weep. I couldn't bear the pain that they would feel coming home, finding Luke and Ryan, hearing that I had been taken. I never wanted to cause anyone I loved pain.

"It's all right. You are going to be alright." She tried to calm me down.

"How can you sit here and tell me that it's all right, that I'm going to be all right? You've been missing for twenty-some odd years, and now they have taken me, and you want me to *calm down*! Do you know what this means?" I shouted in fear.

"So you do know who I am," she said, not responding to my little outburst.

"Yes."

"Then you know what I can do, what we can do?"

"Yes."

"Well then, you already know how I can tell you that it's all right, that you are going to be all right."

"If they have you, what do they want with me?" I asked, terrified and thinking that I probably didn't really want to know the answer. In the TV shows, when the bad guy kidnap two people, one of those people usually ends up dead, and I wasn't exactly ready to die or be the reason someone else dies.

"They want you because my gift is a mere fraction of what yours will become," she told me in a modest voice.

"How is that possible?"

"What my brothers did long ago was brave and wise. It was truly noble of them, trying to rebuild the guardians. What my brothers didn't know was that they weren't the first to have children with a mortal. Before our time, there was another, Annette. She fell in love with a man and soon conceived a child. Annette died in childbirth, leaving her daughter, your mother, without any idea of who she was or of what her bloodline held," she explained to me.

"I still don't understand. How would that make my gift any stronger than yours? By my account, that would still only make me a third guardian, and I know I'm not great at math, but I'm almost positive that a third is less than a whole."

"Do you know your grandfather, Cheveyo?" she asked.

"No, he died before I was born. My mom tells me stories, and I have a picture of him that she gave me. She said his name was Chevy and that he was a great man." I shrugged, not knowing where she was going with any of this.

"Yes, a great man indeed. Though not a guardian, he was a prestigious warrior. Your grandfather was a great Indian man that had many powers of his own."

A great warrior? I hadn't heard these stories before. I thought that perhaps she was confused. *Didn't most of the Indians die out a long time ago?*

She continued with her story, interrupting my thoughts. "Rachel, it is the Indian in you that will make your powers greater than imaginable, vaster than mine. You see, it was thought that Indians could communicate with the world and all of their surroundings. That they could talk to the animals and the dead. That they could communicate with nature. When you harness your blood right, you will be able to see the future, talk to the dead and the animals, and communicate with nature itself. They plan on controlling you and, in doing so, controlling your powers. We can't allow them to control your powers like they have mine for all these years. If they do, the shift in the natural balance would be too great. The world would go into chaos."

Hmm. She doesn't seem to know about my telekinesis. How odd. I would've thought she could see something like that. "What do we do?" I asked. I was ready to be done with all of this. I just wanted to go home.

"We? Rachel, no, this isn't our job. Protecting us and fighting is the job of the other guardians. It is their job to stop the evil. That is what their gifts are meant for, what they are meant for," she told me in an apathetic tone.

"I'm sorry? We do nothing? Ma'am, I may be new to this and all. I may not know exactly how everything works yet, but I can't and won't just sit by while the ones I love risk everything trying to rescue me. They may just be pawns in the grand scheme to you, but to me they are my family and friends, and the way I was raised, family stands up and fights for one another," I told her in a rather harsh tone.

"Then you will die," she told me rather apathetically again. *What is with this woman and not caring if people die?*

"Why am I here?" I asked, finding some composure. I was ready to kill her myself. How can anyone be so cold?

"I brought you here, Rachel. You needed to know what you are up against. I saw this as the only way. I'm sorry."

9

I went and sat down alone in a corner to think. I had to figure out a way to get out of here, and I was sick of listening to anything she had to say. What did she mean she brought me here? If she was so worried about them controlling me, why did she bring me here? Luke told me he would always find me, but how could he? He had no way of knowing where I was or even how to get to me. This wasn't the woods by my house. Who knew how far those things had taken me.

I cleared my head of everything. I thought in detail about all the things around me. About the hard cold, wet rock floors and walls, about the running water, about Madeline. I wondered if I was to be trapped here like her for the rest of my life, if I would ever see my parents or Luke and his family again. Slowly, the more I thought, the faster the tears came.

I wanted to go home. I wanted to be in my nice, safe warm house with my family and friends.

Through blurred vision, I noticed the boulder blocking my escape start to slowly move; quickly, I dried my tears and stood up on shaky legs, smashing myself as far into the wall as I could. I had high hopes that if I made myself small enough, they wouldn't find me. When it was finally moved, a tall dark-haired man with the palest skin I've ever seen stood in the opening. I recognized him from some of the visions I've had. In that instant, I realized that all the monsters in my fairy tales, on TV, and in movies weren't fiction—they were real. The furry beast that had taken me was a werewolf, the woman that looked like Brooke was a shape shifter, and the man that now stood before me was a vampire. A sudden chill ran down my spine as things started to make some sense, but if I were to be truthful, I already knew these things to be real. I just didn't want to admit it.

"Ah, Ms. Rachel Clissdale, it's so very nice to meet you finally. I've waited so long," the vampire addressed me.

"Well, I can't say the same," I hissed back at him.

"Yes, well, where are my manners? I'm Jason, and you've already met Brad, my werewolf friend, and the beautiful shape shifter, Kaylee," he introduced them as they entered the chamber. "Now, Rachel, if you would be so kind as to come with us, we have a lot of work to do," Jason said as Brad grabbed me.

I tried to fight back. "Let go of me! I'm not going anywhere with you. Stop! Let go of me!" I protested, struggling to get free.

"Leave her alone, Jason. She's only a child—" Madeline tried to say but was interrupted suddenly when she hit the floor in convulsions. *What the hell happened to her?*

Brad dragged me out of the room, with me kicking and screaming the whole time. The three of them walked together, dragging me along. Finally, we came into a large chamber with a chair. Brad threw me into the chair and quickly locked my wrist and ankles in the shackles that were attached. I struggled against them. I could feel them cutting into my skin, but I refused to concede to them. There was no way I was just going to let them do God knows what to me without fighting it.

"Rachel, you saw what happened back there to Madeline," Jason said, drawing my attention to him. "So you understand this when I tell you that it is in your best interest not to fight us."

I awoke, suddenly screaming out in pain. Luke was shaking me gently. Scared and confused, I glanced around the room. Everyone was there—my mom, dad, Mark, Clair, Ryan, Luke, and Nathan. They were all staring at me. I started to hyperventilate as tears cascaded down my face. I was safe. *What in the hell is going on? How did I get back here?*

"Rachel! Rachel!" Luke jostled me again, forcing me to look at him, doing my best to acknowledge that I heard him. "Are you okay? What's going on?"

I closed my eyes and did my best to control my breathing. I felt like reality had been ripped out from under me. I understood it must have been a vision, but I didn't understand how that was possible. I had never had one like that before.

"Okay, okay, Rachel, calm down. It's okay, you're okay," Luke told me, taking me into his arms and rocking me while kissing my head.

I could see the alarm in his eyes. I could feel the fear in the room; the tension was almost palpable. Everyone was scared and worried, and no one knew what was going on, not even me. I tried to push Luke away, but I couldn't. My arms, my legs, my whole body hurt, and I couldn't get my voice to work. The more I struggled, the tighter he held me, which made me suddenly scream out in pain. Luke jumped across the room, not understanding what he had done. Without his arms around me holding me, my body fell backward, hitting the pillow on the couch. The sudden movement caused my shirt to lift slightly, showing my lower stomach. I could hear the echoing gasps around the room, but I was too frightened to look at what they saw.

They needed answers, and I knew this. I just had to figure out what I was going to tell them or, better yet, how to explain what happened. My mind was still trying to figure out how I got back here in the first place. It was a very scary feeling to be one place one second and another the next. Slowly I sat up. I knew I was going to have to explain, but I needed answers too.

"What is everyone doing here?" I asked, pulling my shirt back down. I would deal with that later.

It was Ryan who answered me. "Your parents came home and found you collapsed in the kitchen. I guess they called us right after, and here we are. Now it's your turn. What's going on?" he rushed; I'm sure he wanted his own answers.

"I'm not sure. I had a vision, I guess. It had to have been, but I didn't know it at the time. I thought it was reality. Everything to me was very real. I don't know how to explain it. I just don't know. I'm so confused," I said, starting to panic a little.

It was my mom that came to the rescue for once. "It's okay, sweetie. Take your time and just try to explain it the best you can, okay?" I nodded, took a deep breath, and spent the next fifteen minutes explaining everything I saw and heard and answering questions.

I explained to them what I remembered, doing my best to figure out what really happened and what was apart of the vision. I remember walking in the woods with the boys, and after Luke confirmed this, I knew it really happened. Unfortunately the rest of the time I was alone, so all I could really do was guess. I assumed that the vision started while I was making dinner. However my parents informed me that no food was out but that they did find me in the kitchen.

"Okay, but I don't get it. From the looks of your stomach and shoulder, you got pretty roughed up, but from what you said, they didn't lay a finger on you really," Ryan pointed out.

"Yeah, well, the shoulder is easy. You shot me, at least in the vision. Everything else I'm not too sure about myself. I know my whole body hurts, but I can't tell you what happened other than being strapped to a chair."

"Wait wait wait. Back up. I shot you?" Ryan asked.

"Well, you weren't aiming for me, but yeah, you shot me."

"Okay then, I guess," Ryan said sounding a little sad.

"So they are coming for you?" my dad asked.

"No, I don't think so. Not yet at least. I think this was Madeline's way of showing me what we are up against. A warning."

"Okay, Rachel, I think that's enough for right now. Do you think you can make it upstairs so I can take a look at you?" Clair asked.

"I'm not sure," I said, trying to stand up, which took more effort than I'd like to admit.

Once I was finally on my feet, I knew there was no way I was going to be able to make it up the stairs, at least not on my own. I felt exhausted and weak. Before I could say anything, Luke had come over and cradled me in his arms.

"It's okay, baby, I got you."

Careful not to jostle me too much, Luke carried me upstairs to my room, followed by his mom. Clair was a nurse and currently attending medical school to become a doctor. I was happy she was here. I could just see trying to explain all this in an actual ER. I wonder if they'd buy the story that I fell down the stairs. That's always what the abused victims used to say on TV when they were hurt, right?

Once in my room, Clair got to work. "Luke, help me take her pants and shirt off so I can see how bad the injuries are."

"Um, I think you and I can handle this, Clair," I said, terrified of Luke doing this in front of his mom. I might die of embarrassment. *Tonight on News at 9, local teen dies of embarrassment when boyfriend removes her clothes in front of his mother.*

"You can try, sweetie. I was just trying to cause you as little pain as possible. If you think that you can remove your clothes, that's fine. I can understand you not wanting Luke's help."

I nodded my understanding and reached for the button on my jeans. So far so good, button undone and no pain. Now to just start pulling them down. "Ow ow ow!" I whined as I started to wiggle them over my butt.

"It's okay, babe. I'll help. I can close my eyes if it makes you feel better," Luke said, quickly coming to my rescue.

"Oh, shut up," I grumbled embarrassed.

Huh. This is not exactly the way I pictured Luke taking my clothes off for the first time. Okay, so I'm not embarrassed by my body—not in the least. I know I look good, but couldn't my mom help with something like this? I wouldn't mind Luke seeing me in my underwear, but I would really prefer it if his mom wasn't in the room too. Luke looked up from removing my jeans and smiled at me, a smile that quickly turned into a look of horror once they had my clothes off. I didn't have to look to know my body must be in pretty bad shape. *God, I hope that look is because of injuries and not disgust.* My whole body was black and blue with dried blood from cuts and scratches. On my wrist and ankles, there were perfect two-inch half circles from my restraints, and my right shoulder had a nice five-inch gash in it where the bullet nicked me. I knew it was going to need stitches I just hoped Clair was able to take care of it here. Clair and I could both tell Luke was uncomfortable with the sight of me like this. I felt so bad for him. I wouldn't know what I would do if I saw him like this.

"Rachel, sweetie, do you have a sewing kit, rubbing alcohol, gauze, and Neosporin? I'm going to need it to get you all fixed up," Clair asked.

"Yeah, they're in the bathroom, first drawer on the left."

"Great. Luke, can you go get them for me, and ask Trish for some vodka. Then why don't you go downstairs and wait with everyone else," Clair said.

Luke didn't say anything. He just simply nodded and left to get what Clair needed. He was back in seconds and gone again.

"Vodka?" I asked Clair with a puzzled look.

"Yes, it's for you to drink. I don't condone underage drinking, but seeing as how I don't have anything else to numb the pain, it's going to have to work for now," she said, handing me the bottle. "Chug as much as you can, sweetie."

I nodded and chugged what I could before gagging. "Oh god, that is so gross." My throat and stomach burned with the flames of the vodka. *Why do people do this to themselves?*

"I know, sweetie. I'm so sorry, but this is going to hurt." Clair told me as she started working on my shoulder.

I grabbed my pillow, biting into it to keep from screaming. It felt like hours had passed, but I knew it had only been minutes when Clair finally spoke again, "All right, it's clean. I'm going to start stitching it up now. It's going to hurt like hell. I'm sorry. Are you okay?"

"Oh yeah, I'm great. This is better than Disneyland." I said rolling my eyes.

"I know...just try not to think about it." She told me, shaking her head at my antics. *Was I being melodramatic?* I didn't think I was.

It felt so strange. I've had stitches before, but I was always numb. This time, I could feel everything. I felt the needle enter my skin and the thread pull it back together. I was not sure when she finished the stitches. I guess I passed out from the pain. When I woke back up, Clair was calmly sitting next to me, wiping the sweat from my face. I noticed the rest of my cuts had been cleaned and bandaged. I wondered how long I was out.

"Are you ready to continue?" Clair asked.

"As ready as I'm going to be. Sorry for passing out," I said sheepishly. Maybe I can't do this. Maybe Madeline was right. I closed my eyes, trying to push away those thoughts. They wouldn't do me any good, and with those thoughts came the thought of losing everyone I love.

"Okay, I'm going to start with your limbs first. What I'm going to do is ask you to wiggle them and check, the best I can without an x-ray, for broken bones. I don't see any swelling, so you should be fine. Once that's finished, I'm going to lightly press on your belly. By judging your pain, I should be able to tell if there are any internal injuries, I hope."

Once I had nodded my understanding, the rest of my torture began.

Clair started with the fingers on my left hand, then my right, then down to my legs and feet. Then she moved on pushing on my stomach. She softly pushed on my tummy while staring at my face, looking for even the smallest indication of pain. I've had something similar done at the doctor's office lots of times. We were almost done when she lightly pushed on the right side of my ribs, causing me to scream out in pain. Not five seconds later, people flooded up the stairs; from my room, they sounded like a stampeding herd of animals.

Clair stood up as they entered my room. "I don't believe there are any broken bones or internal injuries, but it does appear that she has bruised her ribs. It's a perfectly harmless injury. However, it's going to hurt like hell for a couple of weeks. Rachel, you need to take it easy until they're healed so that you don't cause any more damage to them. Other than that, it appears to be surface wounds, and they should heal before your ribs do."

I nodded, accepting my diagnoses, thankful for it. I suppose it could've been a lot worse. I carefully stood up and went to my closet for some comfy, clean clothes. I should have been embarrassed at everyone seeing me in only my panties and bra, but I was in too much pain to care, and I was pretty sure I was a little drunk from the vodka. Everyone just stood there staring at me in horror. Glancing at my mom, I could see the fear in her eyes and what looked like tears. I wondered if I looked as bad as I felt. While getting dressed, I tried to push all fears and doubts from my mind. I needed to appear strong and in control, at least for a little longer.

"Okay. So what's the plan? What are we going to do?" I quickly asked once my clothes were on and I had gathered my thoughts.

No one answered me. No one even moved a muscle. They all just stood there frozen.

"Come on, guys. I'm fine. I'll be fine. You heard what Clair said, surface wounds and bruised ribs. I've had worse from cheer. You had to have known that it was possible, that something like this might happen one day," I said, looking at my dad and Mark.

They didn't have to say anything; I could see it all written plainly on their faces. They had thought something like this might happen one day. It was clear my dad had tried to prepare himself for it. Even now I could see the determination in his eyes. Granted, it was also clear that they hadn't prepared themselves properly, at least not for the way that it had happened. I think they were prepared to come home and find out I had been taken, to fight a deadly war to get me back. But instead, my powers took over, or Madeline's powers, giving me a glimpse of what we were to face. I knew we needed action. I felt like the time for standing by had passed. Even with how bad I felt, I was ready to grab my pitchfork and go monster hunting.

"We have plenty of time for this, sweetie. Why don't you just lie down and try to get some rest?" my dad finally managed to spit out through clenched teeth. I don't think I've ever seen my father so angry. At least he isn't angry with me.

I stared at him with my mouth hanging open for a good five minutes. *Did he really think I could rest after the things I had just learned and saw?* No, I wanted to make plans, take action, and fight back! "Rest? You want me to rest? How can I rest when there are monsters out there trying to kill my family and take me?" I was losing control over my anger again, and that never seemed to end well.

"Rachel, sweetie, it has always been our job to protect the foresight. We failed with Madeline, but we won't fail when it comes to you. I promise. Let us do what we do, sweetie," Mark told me with what looked like tears in his eyes. It was difficult to see such sorrow on his face.

I finally think I understood. It wasn't so much that they didn't want me to fight. I think it was more honor to them. They had failed Madeline and were scared of failing me. There was so much more on the line this time.

I sighed and took a deep breath. "Can I speak with my dad and Mark alone please?" I asked. I needed them to understand I wasn't Madeline and neither were my powers. However, I couldn't expect them to just know these things.

I was going to have to find a way to show them, prove it to them that I could help. I just wasn't sure how to do that.

Once everyone was out of my room except my dad and Mark, I sat down on my bed and closed my eyes. "Madeline said my powers are stronger than hers and different," I told them while concentrating on the monsters, hoping that it would help me get angry. When I could feel my anger bubbling inside, I finally opened my eyes to look at them. "I want to help." This whole having to get angry is starting to make me feel like the Hulk.

"Rachel, I understand that, but, sweetie, you're my only child, and I couldn't live with myself if anything happened to you," my dad said honestly for the first time.

"Nothing will happen to me," I told him, carefully using my anger to push him into the wall. I wanted to show him my powers, not hurt him. Unfortunately, I wasn't exactly sure how to use them yet myself, so I had to be careful. I doubt it would help me prove my point at all if I lost control.

"Rachel, how are you doing that?" Mark asked as my dad struggled to get away from the wall.

"I don't know. I've been able to move small things since I was about four. Only recently have I been able to move large things, and I'm still trying to figure out how it all works," I explained, letting my dad go. "I know I have to be angry and seeing as how it tends to be kind of destructive, I haven't exactly played around with it too much yet."

"Rachel, you could control the world, it doesn't matter what you show me, my answer is still going to be no. You will not be fighting. You are my only daughter, my only child. What would I do if something happened to you, if I let something happen to you? Not to mention what it would do to your mother," my dad said. He shook his head, turned and walked out of my room.

"So you can all fight and die for me, but I can't?" I screamed at his back. I was furious.

"This is no longer up for discussion, Rachel. You are to tell us if you are seeing anything, anything at all. Am I understood?" my dad yelled as he came back and stood right inside the doorway.

"I won't let you all die for me," I said, losing all control. I could feel all this rage building inside me, and then it just felt like it exploded out of my chest. Every window in the house broke, and I heard the doors slam. I heard my mom and Clair scream downstairs, and the boys come running up. My dad and Mark both just stood there, staring at me.

"What happened?" Luke asked, being the first into my room.

I couldn't take this, any of it. I could feel my anger rolling through me like a rough sea. "Get out!" I screamed, throwing one of my hands up, pushing Luke and his brothers out of my room even though they weren't close enough for me to reach. I watched as they went flying backward out of my room, and the door slammed behind them. I was on autopilot. I was angry, and I guess my brain knew how to use my powers even if I didn't. "I will *not* stand by while you give your lives for mine. I am not just some child!" I screamed at my father, pushing him back into a wall again.

"Rachel, you need to calm down. I understand that you're angry, and I understand why, but you don't want to hurt your dad," Mark told me.

I took a deep breath, doing my best to release my anger. "Just go, do what you want. Just don't expect me to sit by while you all go and kill yourselves," I told my dad as my tears started to fall.

"Rachel."

"No, Daddy, just go, please," I asked, curling into a ball and crying on my bed. I heard him sigh as he and Mark left my room and closed my door.

10

I could hear the fears and doubts in my head. I was my own worst enemy. *What if Madeline was wrong? What if they all died? What if I wasn't as strong as I thought I was? What if it's all my fault?* The more I thought, the harder I cried. Eventually, I must've cried myself to sleep, but I couldn't escape my fears even in my dreams. Images of blood, mangled bodies, and funerals swirled through my mind, causing me to wake up scared.

I had no idea how long I had been asleep, but what I did know was that my dad was wrong; we didn't have plenty of time. These things were coming, and we needed to have a plan. I could sense the answers to the questions I had been asking myself for most of my life forming inside me. So much of what had me stumped for so long was finally beginning to make sense, but how did I know these things?

That isn't important, I told myself, trying not to allow my mind to wander. I needed to focus on my impending doom. *Okay, so it wasn't an attack. No, it was a warning sent to me from Madeline*, I thought in a brutal attempt to understand the feelings rushing through me. Adam's death hadn't been a mere animal attack; I had always been positive of that. Granted it's not like they could just come out and say that it was a vampire, but I doubted the authorities knew that's what had happened to begin with. My thoughts raced; they had gotten to him in a futile attempt at getting to me. I was the "her" they spoke of. They had turned him against me. They were hoping to lure me to their side using him, and when it had become apparent to them that I would no longer follow Adam, they killed him. That's why my dad had been so focused on the "her." He already knew they were after me. I wonder how much if any of this my family had already figured out. A sudden terrifying thought flashed in my mind. *Had all of those people been hurt because of me?* Taking a deep breath, I pushed it away again. I couldn't handle being the reason so many people were hurt and killed.

A sudden unease fell on me as all of my thoughts finally came together. My family had known all along that this fight was coming, and from what Luke had said, they had to have known it was coming soon. *Why am I just now figuring all of this out? Why would they keep this from me? Why do they keep everything from me?*

I slowly stood up and carefully walked out of my room to the bathroom. I wanted to shower. I still felt gross from earlier. Carefully I peeled off my clothes and looked in the mirror at my body for the first time. I looked like a car had run me over. Everything seemed as if it had at least a light bruising to it. I shook my head, ignoring the current state my body was in. I had to figure all this out. I knew from my fairy tale and from Madeline's warning that I was our best defense. There had to be a way for me to figure it out and understand how to fight them, how to win.

Once I was out of my shower and dressed, I sat on my bed with my eyes closed, thinking. I thought about my grandfather, Chevy, and of my grandmother, Annette. I knew the answers I needed were here. I just had to find them.

"Yes, Rachel, brains you have. But strength, speed, and grace—these you also possess," a voice I had never heard before told me.

My eyes shot open, scanning my room for the man that had spoken the words. A small gasp escaped my lips as my eyes locked gazes with a man sitting in my rocking chair, a man I had only ever seen before in pictures.

"Grandpa?"

"Why do you sound so surprised, sweetie? You are the one who called on me."

"I did?"

"Rachel, you have the strength and the gifts of the most dominant bloodlines in history. Sweetie, never take that for granted, and never forget the strength that comes from love. Love is the most powerful force when possessed in the proper ways. It is kind, caring, never judging, and bliss, but it is also harsh, strong, graceful, and holds immense speed. A speed that you and I have both witnessed. You, when you met Luke, and me, when I met your grandmother, Annette. Once we laid our eyes upon them, we changed. Do you know any other feeling that can cause a person to change so fast? The love that we felt for them consumed us so completely we no longer breathed merely because we had to, and from that moment, every breath we took was for them. Rachel, evil calls upon fear in order to win battles. Fear is very strong. It also swiftly consumes one if they allow it, but, my sweet child, it cannot win the war. The war, this war you will win through love. Allow it to consume you entirely, empower you, to fuel your powers."

"But I don't know how."

"Yes, you do, Rachel. I'm always with you, watching over you. Let go of your fear and allow the love you feel to replace it."

"How do I let go of the fear? I don't want to be alone. I can't be the reason they all die," I said with tears in my eyes.

"You won't be."

"How can you be so sure of everything when I'm sure of nothing?"

"Because I am, sweetie. I've watched you since you were a baby. You have doubts about yourself, but I have none."

I nodded and closed my eyes, attempting to let go of the fear I was feeling; when I opened them, he was gone. "Thanks, Grandpa," I whispered to nothing.

I sat there for a while, just staring at my rocking chair. *I can do this*, I told myself. *Not that I had much of a choice in the matter.* When I snapped out of my daze and back to reality, it felt like it had only been minutes, but it must have been hours because I could hear everyone downstairs cooking and talking. Looking out my window, I could see the sun rising. I had managed to sit in the same position on my bed for the rest of the night. I had no idea how I had managed that as I lay down, stretching out my back and legs. Suddenly I heard a light knock at my door. It was Ryan.

"Hey, chica, can I come in?"

"Huh? Oh yeah, sure, come on in. What's up? What are you still doing here?"

I asked rolling over on my bed to look at him. *What could he possibly want?*

"Well, thanks to someone, we've been up all night putting boards where windows used to be," Ryan said, looking at me pointedly.

"Oops." I shrugged. "Mine isn't done."

"Yeah, that's because when we came in here to do yours, you were asleep, and no one would let us wake you. Personally, I think you deserved to be woken up. You were a pretty big brat last night."

"What do you want, Ryan?" I growled.

"Can we talk?"

Can we talk? Great, nothing good ever comes from those words. Haven't we been talking? "Sure. What about?" I asked, hoping my expression didn't give away the unease I was feeling at this moment.

"About your dream or vision or whatever it was."

"Umm…yeah, sure, but I thought I covered it all pretty well last night. What is it exactly that you want to know?"

"Yeah, you did. I just wanted some more details. You know me. I just want to know whose ass I'm going to be kicking so I can make sure to take names." He smiled at me. "So did you see anyone else? Maybe someone you forgot to mention?"

Sighing, I did my best to answer his question. "It started with you and Luke fighting with a werewolf and a shape-shifter. Eventually, they got me and took me back to some type of cave or something where they kept me. I met Madeline, and then suddenly a vampire named Jason was there introducing his goon squad, Brad and Kaylee, the werewolf and shape-shifter. Pretty much that's it."

"Oh…okay, so that's all? I mean, you didn't meet anyone else?"

"No. Was there someone else that I was supposed to have met? 'Cause frankly, I didn't want to meet the ones that I did." *What kind of questions are these? What is going on with him? Who did he think I met?* I was getting a strange vibe, but I had no clue what was going on.

"No, no. I just figured by the way everyone was talking that there was more. I mean, really, two little guys and a chick? What's everyone so worried about? I could take them in my sleep."

"Ryan, I am sure that Jason has an army on his side, but we didn't exactly play meet and great."

"Okay, well let's get you downstairs for breakfast. You are going to need it to heal. By the way has anyone told you yet?"

"Told me what?"

"Chica, you look like hell."

"Thanks, Ryan, you really know how to make a girl feel special," I said, rolling my eyes at him.

"What can I say? I do what I can." He smiled his big goofy grin at me. I shook my head, chuckling as I got out of bed.

Downstairs, the table was set, and everyone was already seated as we made our way to the only open spots. We all sat there eating our breakfast quietly. Everyone was staring at me, and I was starting to lose my patience. I hated when people stared at me. It was nothing drastic or anything; it's just every time I looked up from my food, one person was looking at me. *What did they want me to say? Did they want me to apologize?* That's when a really scary thought occurred to me: *Are they afraid of me?* Luke reached for my hand, holding it, soothing all my nerves.

"It's okay. We just don't know what to say, babe. You kind of threw us all for a loop last night."

My head dropped in disappointment; I knew I had scared everyone, most importantly Luke. I hadn't meant to. It's not like I had any control over any of it. "I'm sorry. I didn't mean to scare anyone." Granted, I did manage to break every window in the house.

"Oh god, Rachel, we know you didn't, but we are all trying to wrap our heads around it as I am sure you are as well," Clair explained.

I nodded. "Yes, ma'am. May I please be excused?" I asked politely. I got up from the table and returned my plate to the kitchen.

"Rachel, are you okay?" my dad asked. He had followed me out of the room.

What was I supposed to say? Am I okay? Really? What I thought to be real, actually isn't and what I thought I knew to be make believe is actually real… oh you know and trying to kill my family and me. *Yup, I'm just dandy.* Thankfully all of that didn't come out. "Yeah, Daddy, I'm fine. Just a little tired and not very hungry. I think I am going to try and take a nap. Maybe a hot bath." Thankfully, he accepted this answer because I didn't know what else to say.

Slowly I walked upstairs and into my room. I wanted to be alone, away from everyone. I couldn't deal with my nerves and theirs. I wanted to discuss and plan what was going to happen, how, and when. But no one else seemed thrilled about talking about it. At least not with me. I guess I should be used to this by now. I lay on my bed, staring up at my ceiling, trying to figure everything out. *Why is this happening? None of this can be real. I have to be dreaming, right?* I pinched myself. "Ouch." Nope, not dreaming. *Well, great, now what am I going to do? I said it last night, I'm not Madeline. I feel like that's all I've been saying since I figured all this out. I'm nowhere close to her and all of her power. How am I going to be able to help my family?* The thoughts and worries ran through my head until eventually I fell asleep, but even that wasn't restful. I tossed and turned as my battered body ached. I was chased by my fears. Abruptly, I sat up in my bed, looking around. My heart was pounding, and I could feel the cool glisten of sweat all over me. I felt like I was going crazy until finally my eyes landed on Luke.

"Hey. Sorry, sweetie, I didn't mean to wake you, but we needed to get a board over your window. Your dad called and ordered new windows. They should be here Monday," Luke told me.

"Great, thanks," I said, lying back down and rolling over to face away from him.

"Rachel, what's wrong?"

"Nothing, I'm fine."

"Really? That's the answer you're going to give me? Okay, well, we both know that's a lie. Let me know when you're ready to talk."

"What do you want me to say, Luke? That I feel like I'm going crazy? That there is no way any of this can be real. That I feel like I can't escape even in my dreams. Please tell me because right now I feel hopeless and lost," I said sitting up as tears started to fall softly.

"Rachel, everything is going to be fine. I told you we have trained our whole lives for this. We won't let anything happen to you," Luke said, sitting down and holding me.

"Get away from me," I said, sending him flying to the other side of the room with one motion of my hand. Thankfully, Luke was much better at all of this than I was; he spun in the air and caught himself before he went flying into the wall. "Oh my god, I'm so sorry. I didn't mean to," I said, breaking down again.

"Why are you mad at me?" Luke asked, coming to sit back on my bed, away from me this time.

"I'm not," I told him, looking up from my bed.

Luke didn't say anything in return; he just gave me this "you've got to be kidding me" look.

"I don't know. I try talking to you guys, and all anyone ever says is 'Don't worry, we've got this,' but I do worry. I'm not scared to die. Why can't any of you see that? I'm scared of being left alone. I've died a thousand times in my visions. Death will never scare me, but to lose you, my dad, everyone…I don't know how to do that. Still you all seem so willing to die for me, for the world. How is that okay? Why? Why should I be the one that has to give up everything? I know I sound selfish, but you all have known what you are and what you can do your whole lives. I've only just figured any of this out on my own, might I add, and now I feel like

I'm going to lose you all. Luke, I can't lose anyone. I'm not strong enough for that."

"Rachel, you get mad because we are nonchalant about it. We don't think we will die, but why are you so sure we will?"

"Because when I sit down and try to see it, all I ever see is death," I told him simply.

"Then you need to tell Dad and Peter. They need to know. They have to figure something else out."

"But my dad won't listen to me. Don't you think I've been trying?"

"No, you've been trying to get him to let you fight. That isn't going to happen. But if the way we plan to fight them isn't going to work, then we need to know so we can change it."

"Guys, lunch!" I heard my mom call up the stairs.

"Come on, let's go eat. We can talk to them together after lunch," Luke told me, grabbing my hand.

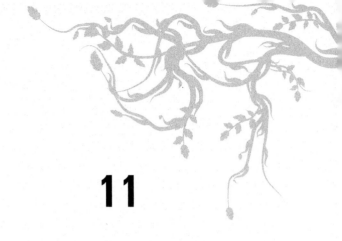

11

Lunch was a quick meal. The guys scarfed their food before it ever hit their plates, I think. Not that I was one to talk. Having skipped breakfast this morning, I was starving. When I had finished with my food, I stood to put my plate away.

"Rachel?" my dad called out to me.

"Yes?"

"I want you to go pack a bag for the night."

"Why? Where am I going?"

"Well, your mother and I discussed it, and with everything going on and us not having any windows, we think it would be best if you stayed with Mark, Clair, and the boys tonight."

"What about you and mom?"

"We're going to stay here and get everything cleaned up."

"I can stay and help."

"No, sweetie, you need to heal."

"Okay." I nodded and headed upstairs. I could've argued, but I was tired. I felt like I hadn't slept in weeks.

All I wanted to do was go back to sleep and pretend all of this was a dream. But I knew eventually, I would wake back up and undoubtedly have to face my new reality, assuming it didn't chase me into my dreams. I sighed as I turned on the faucet to take a shower. What was I going to do? They wouldn't let me fight, and I didn't know how to keep them from dying. Before I could step into the shower, the vision hit me like a ton of bricks.

I was downstairs in the living room surrounded by my family. It was insane how quick we were surrounded by them; they were everywhere. I stood there frozen to the spot, watching in horror. We were severely outnumbered ten to one. I knew there was no way we could possibly fight our way out of this, but I had no idea what to do. It was a gruesome sight as I saw four vampires converge on Clair, biting all the flesh they could get their fangs into. I turned away, unable to watch as they killed her, but it didn't matter where I looked—people I loved were dying all around me. To my left, my mom was being torn apart by werewolves. Two had her arms and two had her legs, and they were pulling in different directions. To my right, Mark was putting up a good fight against three werewolves and two vampires, I watched as he transported from one spot to the next trying to evade them, but without weapons, he was only postponing the inevitable. I turned away, looking for my dad; he would know what to do, but I didn't find him. Instead, I found Luke. He was pinned down by ten werewolves struggling to get to what I assumed was his lighter. Without it, his powers wouldn't work. However he was too outnumbered and quickly losing the battle, and before I could look away, one ripped his head from his shoulders.

"No!" I screamed, collapsing to the bathroom floor. They were all going to die. Taking a deep breath, I gathered my resolve and stood up. I had to tell the guys what I had seen. They needed to know. I had to warn them. Forgetting about my shower, I threw my clothes back on and ran downstairs. As I was turning into the living room, the vision hit me again. Body pieces were everywhere; I couldn't catch my breath as Jason grabbed me.

"Stop!" I screamed, snapping out of the vision again.

Looking around at my family, I was struck by déjà vu: everyone was dressed the same as the vision. They were coming now.

"Rachel?" my dad asked, coming to me. "Are you okay? Sweetie, you're bleeding."

"Dad, they're coming."

"I know, sweetie. I told you we will take care of everything."

"No, Dad! They're coming *now*!" I screamed in a panic. "I've seen it. You have to do something now, or you all will die." They stood there for much longer than they should have, staring at me.

"Luke, take Rachel. Get into your car and drive. Don't stop until we call you. Do you understand?" my dad told him.

"Yes, sir," Luke said, grabbing my hand and pulling me toward the door.

"No," I said, struggling out of his grasp. "I'm not going anywhere until I know all of you will be safe."

"For god's sake, Rachel, we don't have time for this. We are going to Mark's, but we have no way of knowing if they will see that coming. Now go!"

In a flash, Luke and I were in his car and on the road out of town.

"Where are we going?" I asked, looking at Luke.

"As far away from here as we can get."

I sighed, turning to look out the window; I watched as the trees flew by. I had no idea where we were going, and I had no clue if my family would be okay. I tried to take deep breaths; a panic attack right now wouldn't do me any good.

"Are you okay?"

"No," I said, the word barely escaping my mouth.

"Rachel, they'll be okay, I promise."

"How can you promise me that when you don't know it for sure?"

"Because they have to be," Luke told me, grabbing my hand.

We drove for hours, waiting for a call that would tell us they were okay. The more minutes ticked by, the more my panic rose. *What if they were all dead? What was I going to do?* Before I could send myself into a full fledge panic, the phone rang.

"Yeah," Luke answered, putting his phone on speaker.

"We're fine, you can head home now," Mark said before hanging up the phone.

"What now?" I asked, turning to Luke.

"Now we head home and regroup, but first, I've got to find somewhere to pull over and get gas."

"Good, I've gotta pee."

The downside to traveling in the country is that bathrooms and gas stations are far and few between. The good part is you can't beat the view. It's just beautiful landscape after beautiful landscape. It was another half hour before we got to a gas station and a bathroom. Thank God! For the past fifteen minutes, I have been wiggling in my seat trying to hold it.

"Where are you going?" Luke asked as I jumped out of the car before it had fully stopped moving.

"To the bathroom," I said, not bothering to stop.

"Rachel, wait," Luke called out.

"What?"

"From now on you aren't going anywhere alone. Not even the bathroom."

"You've got to be kidding me." By the look on his face, I knew he wasn't. "Argh, whatever, just hurry up."

I couldn't believe it when he stood outside the stall door while I peed. It's very difficult to pee when you have someone waiting for you, listening to everything you do. *What the hell did he think could happen to me in a freaking bathroom?* All of this was all getting to be too much. I could see the future for god's sake; I think I would know if something was going to attack me while on the toilet, which might I add would be very rude.

Finally, we were back on the road and at Luke's before I knew it. My anxiety had been up since the stupid vision; I was ready to see my family and know for myself that they were okay. Again, I was out of the car before it had completely come to a stop.

"Jesus, Rachel, they already called and told us they were fine. What's the rush? Don't tell me you have to pee again," Luke called after me.

"No, but I want to see them for myself," I told him opening the front door. "Mom! Dad!" I called as I walked in. I needed to see them and know they were okay. Thankfully, I didn't have to wait long before everyone was greeting us at the door. "Oh, thank God you're all okay. I was so worried," I said, hugging everyone I could reach.

"Of course we're okay, sweetie," my dad said, hugging me tightly back.

"Did they come here?" Luke asked as he came in.

"No," Mark answered.

"Oh, I hope they didn't mess up my house," my mom said with a frazzled look. Leave it to my mother to be worried about her house.

"You haven't gone back to check?" I asked, confused. If it were me, I would've wanted to see what was done. We absolutely needed to get video surveillance.

"No, sweetie. Mark and I discussed it, and we think it's best if we all stay here for the time being," my dad told me.

"For how long?" I asked.

"Until I feel it's safe for us to go back home."

"Like today? Tomorrow? When?"

"Jesus, Rachel, I don't know. What's so important at home?"

"Oh, you mean besides my life? Let's see…my clothes, shower stuff, makeup, hair products. I have nothing here."

"Oh, sweetie, we can go into town and buy you new clothes. In fact, I think that sounds like a great idea. I think we could all use a break," my mom said, all too happy at the opportunity to go shopping.

"But I don't want to go shopping," I protested.

"Well, thankfully, I didn't ask for your opinion."

"Thanks, Mom." She rolled her eyes.

"So I can't go home, but I can go into town shopping? That doesn't seem like a bad idea to anyone else?" I asked, confused with their logic.

"You'll be safer with Clair and your mom in town shopping than you will be here with all of us." My dad told me.

"How?"

"Because they can sense all of our powers. All of us being together makes it that much easier. But your mom and Clair don't have powers, so see safer." My dad explained as if I were stupid.

"Great." I sighed.

Since clearly I didn't have a choice in the matter, Clair, mom, and I piled into Clair's SUV and headed into to town for some girl time and shopping. I would've much rather have stayed at home with the guys, but I didn't get a choice. Not even Luke was on my side when it came to me staying at home. I thought they wanted to protect me. Apparently, big bad things never attack while you're being tortured with shopping. *Great.* So after four hours of shopping and more bags than we could carry, we were finally headed back to Clair's. I still wanted to go home, but at least now I had clothes and everything that I needed, except my books for school, but of course they had a quick fix for that too. Luke and I had all the same classes even though they were at different times, so of course I would just use his books. *Gee, why didn't I think of that?* Yes, I was pouting, but I wanted to go home. Tomorrow was Monday, and that meant back to school. It would be nice to get a good night's rest after the couple of days I've had. Assuming they let me go back to school. I can't say that I was enjoying school the way I used to but at least I had a few classes alone where no one was hovering over me. Once we were back at home, I was sent upstairs to put my things away and get comfortable.

"Put your things in Nathan's room. You'll be bunking with him," my dad told me as I walked in.

"Why Nathan's room? Why can't I stay in one of the guest rooms?"

"Because I don't want you alone in case anything happens."

"Then why can't I stay with Luke?"

"Because you're seventeen-year-olds and I'm not stupid."

"But, Dad, it's not like that."

"I don't care. Nathan's room."

"Jesus, fine! And just so you know, he's a guy with a penis too," I shouted, heading upstairs to put away all my new crap.

"Lord, Rachel," my dad said, shaking his head and apologizing for my behavior.

Why did I need to be watched? I could handle myself. What did they think was going to happen to me? Okay, so I knew what they thought was going to happen to me, but I was in a house full of supernatural beings that were there to protect me. How much trouble could I possibly get into while I slept?

"I know you're not happy with the sleeping arrangements. I'm sorry," Nathan said, standing at the door with a bunch of blankets and pillows. "You can take the bed. I'll sleep on the floor." He said sitting the blankets down by the door.

"No, it's your room. It's bad enough I'm taking it over with all my crap. You can at least have your bed."

"As long as you're comfortable, that's all that matters," Nathan told me. I couldn't help it; I just stood there staring at him. *What's wrong with him? Why is he so kind?* I envied that about him. It just wasn't me. "Dinner will be ready soon." He turned to go back downstairs.

"Thanks," I called after him. *Man, I feel like a horrible person.* Was I really being that selfish? I shook my head to try to clear it; I finished putting away my clothes and headed down to help with dinner.

"Rachel, you'll go to school as usual tomorrow, but you are going to ride with Luke and Ryan, and you are to come straight back here after class. No exceptions," my dad told me at dinner.

"Yes, sir."

"Thank you for not arguing for once."

"Would it do me any good?" I asked hopefully.

"No," my dad said, looking disappointed. "You do realize we are all doing this for you, don't you?"

"Yes. May I go to bed, please?"

"Sure," my mom answered. "We love you, sweetie."

"I know, Mom. I love you too."

"Okay, honey, sleep well. We're all here if you need anything."

I nodded and headed upstairs. I felt like crap. I was tired and had a headache from all the anxiety of the day. I quickly changed into pajamas and made a pallet on the floor. I knew I wasn't going to be too comfortable, but I couldn't take Nathan's bed. I just didn't feel right about it. However, I was asleep before my head hit the pillow, so I guess it didn't matter.

Something was after me; I couldn't see it, but I could feel it. I had to get away, find somewhere to hide. It was dark and late. I knew going into the woods wasn't the best of ideas, but I didn't know where else to run. If I would be in the woods, at least they wouldn't find me as easily. I had run forever before I tripped on something, falling to the floor, causing me to wake up. Opening my eyes, I realized I *was* in the woods. *What the hell? How did I get here?* I laid there on the forest floor for what felt like forever, just staring at what few stars I could see through the trees. I wished I could stay here in this feeling. It had been so hard lately; I miss the feeling of bliss. *How had we gotten here? Why did my life have to change?* For the first time in my life, I felt empowered and strong, but I also felt betrayed, confused, and lost. They were odd and confusing feelings, constantly contradicting each other. I felt all over the place, and it was hard to get a handle on what I was feeling. In a matter of days, everything I thought I knew had changed. My entire life had been flipped upside down. To be honest, I would give anything to go back. A year ago, life was perfect. I had the perfect life in the perfect town with the perfect family. Okay, sure they had their own little quirks, but honestly, who didn't? I should be scared, frightened by all my newfound revelations, but oddly I wasn't, not at this moment. I'm not sure I had ever truly felt at peace in my life, but finally

I did. It was amazing what the knowledge of who I was did for me. I mean, I was upset at them for all the things that they had kept from me, things that I felt weren't theirs to keep in the first place. They had neglected to tell me who I was and what I could do, and in doing so, they had not only put me into jeopardy but also everyone I cared so deeply about.

I had to figure out a way to fix this. I am a problem solver; it is who I am, who I have always been. For every problem, there is always a solution. I just had to get to the solution that I could live with in the end. I lay there adrift in the twinkling wonder of the stars for a few moments longer. I was lost in the beauty of the world. At that moment, I wondered if anything in such a beautiful world could honestly ever truly be evil. Perhaps there was no such thing as evil, only misunderstood and misguided people, but then again I suppose the things that were after me weren't human at all, not really.

"You will be mine," the voice was so loud and so close it sent shivers down my spine, causing my dream to come back to me. The panic I felt while asleep was back now, and I rushed to get to my feet and run. I had been running from something. Something was after me. How had I forgotten so easily?

There wasn't much I could do here in the forest, and I knew that, making any hope I had of escape evaporate. *If only they trained me like they did everyone else perhaps, then I can at least protect myself*, I thought shaking my head. I stopped and turned around to face whatever it was that was after me, granted if I was honest I already knew who it was.

"I'm done running. I'm done being afraid. Let's just get this over with. What do you want from me?" I screamed to no one in particular.

"You know that by having Madeline, the balance is in our favor. However, when you learn to control your powers, it will be back in the favor of the Almighty," Jason said, stepping out of the shadows finally. "With you by my side, I will be indestructible."

"So what, you think that by possessing me you will be in the favor of the Almighty? Wow, you are insane. You are an evil creature hell-bent on death and destruction. It doesn't matter who you have on your side. You will not win this fight. If you manage to kill all of us, there will always be more."

"Well, I suppose we shall see," he said, charging at me.

It was just him and me. Granted he was a vampire and I had no weapons of any kind other than my gifts, which I didn't really know how to use, I was screwed. He lunged at me, and in the very last second, I threw myself to the right, barely avoiding him.

Quickly getting back to my feet, I prepared for his next attack. I knew I would have to find a way to get away from him. I wasn't going to be able to outrun him, and I doubted that I would be able to outmaneuver him for long. He came at me again, this time taking his time walking toward me. I could see the calculation in his movements; he was trying his best to anticipate my next move. The problem with this was that I didn't even know my next move. I looked around me and found a tree branch. I grabbed it and brandished it the best I could. I swung out at him and made contact with his gut. He took a few steps back.

I didn't have time to think; instincts took over. I ran at him, hitting him consistently until he was unmoving on the ground. Before I had time to think about it, I dropped the branch and ran as fast as I could toward home. I didn't want to be a hero—I didn't know how to be one. All I wanted was for everyone I loved to survive, and that included me. Looking frantically around, I saw my heaven, I saw home. There right on the other side of the trees, I could make out the glow of the approaching lights. I let out a sigh of relief, knowing that I would soon be back with my family. My legs were tiring quickly as I pushed on. I begged for them to keep up the pace. My only thoughts and concerns now were of me getting out of the forest and into the safe and loving arms of my family. I had one foot on freedom as I was nearing my exit; one more step and I was free, I was home. I knew I hadn't hurt Jason in any real capacity. In the back of my mind, I knew there was no reason I had made it this far; he had to playing with me. I pushed those thoughts back and pushed myself harder. I had to be free of the woods, of this nightmare.

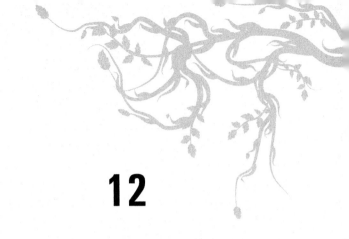

12

"No!" My attempted shout came out as a whimper. "No, please let me go," I begged, tears rolling down my face as I was swept up into his arms. My face pressed against his unbeating heart. My facade was gone now. *Seriously. I'm now begging a vampire to have mercy on me. All of this was unreal. What's wrong with me?* my inner voice questioned. I should be fighting, not crying and begging for mercy. I felt like a failure and helpless as all the fight drained out of me, at least for the moment. *Stop it!* my inner voice screamed. *You have to fight. Find your inner warrior, and get the hell out of this.*

"Now why would I do that, my pet? I have only now gotten you right where I have so longed to have you." The evil that dwelled deep inside his soul was plastered throughout his words. I could hear it, the evil and misdeeds seeping into the air, as he spoke. It made me want to hold my breath for fear that if I breathed it in, it would attach itself to me. I could picture the evil in his voice attacking my soul, my mind, in attempt at corrupting what wasn't his to corrupt.

Hopelessly, I lay there in his arms. I saw no use in struggling; it wouldn't do me any good. As I closed my eyes, I could feel as he started to run with me deeper and deeper into the woods. I sent up silent prayers to a God I hoped was willing to help me. Not that I felt like I had ever done anything in my life worth his help. I needed a way to make him stop. I needed time to make a plan to figure out how to get free, but nothing was coming to me. I knew I had to think fast. The longer we ran, the more hopeless I became. Finally like a thought that wasn't mine, I remembered the cross hanging from my neck. It was a small cross that I had gotten for Christmas last year from my mom, but I had hope that it was enough. Moving as little as I could, I reached up and ripped it from my neck. Holding it in my hand, I looked at it, sending up one final prayer, and stuck the cross to the exposed skin of his neck. He sucked in a breath through his clenched teeth. As he stopped running and dropped me to the ground, the speed in which he stopped sent me flying through the air. I hit the trunk of a nearby tree, knocking the breath out of me. At least it didn't knock me out.

"Very clever, my dear. Very clever indeed. But God cannot save you," he said, looking at me with an amount of rage that I have never before witnessed. If looks could kill, I would surely already be dead.

"He doesn't have to save me, only buy me time," I said, struggling to stand.

"Time for what? You cannot fight me and win. You cannot outrun me. I see no escape for you." He laughed a deep menacing laugh, the ones that you hear in your nightmares. "Come on, Rachel, you've seen this all so many times before. Tell me, how does it always end?"

It was then that I saw just a glimpse of them so fast that it could've just as easily been my imagination, but I had hope and faith. "Perhaps that's because you can't see clearly. I think this time it ends badly for you. Don't you know the bad guys always lose?"

As if they were avenging angels, Luke and Ryan stepped out of the shadows. "She may not be able to fight you, but I'm positive I can handle you," Luke said. "Ryan, take Rachel." Luke stepped closer to Jason, putting himself between the vampire and me. Ryan had me in his arms before I could blink. Relief rushed through me at the sight of them. I was saved, but how did they know how to find me? How did they even know I was gone? I had no idea what time it was, but I had assumed everyone was asleep in the house when I left. I didn't get a chance to ask. We took off toward home, leaving Luke behind.

"No, Ryan! Go back! We can't just leave him there alone!" I ordered, banging on his chest with all the strength I could muster.

He didn't answer; he just kept running. How could he do that? How could he just leave his little brother out there alone? He was all alone; my heart ached knowing that there was no way he would make it home unharmed…if he made it home at all. We hit the edge of the forest, and we were home. Ryan slowed to a quick pace, still racing for his house.

"Ryan, please please please take me back," I tried to beg again, but it was of no use. My pleas were now muffled by the waterfall of tears streaming down my face, and even I couldn't understand what I was saying.

Ryan didn't say anything to anyone as he passed them. I suppose everyone already knew I was gone. I wonder what it must feel like to know they trusted you enough to not be worried when you were up against a vampire. He just kept moving quickly into the house, up the stairs, and into Luke's room, where he finally sat me down on the bed. He quietly shuffled to the corner of the room, watching out the window. He offered me no words or gestures of comfort.

Fear and pain hit me like a tsunami; Luke had come to rescue me, but he stayed to defend me. He stayed alone, why? *Why didn't he tell our families? Why didn't they come as well? What was going on? Why did he have to leave me? How was I going to do this without him?* I couldn't breathe as all my fears rushed to the surface. *Why did he do this? Why was I in the woods in the first place? What do I do now? It's all my fault.* My anxiety was starting to overwhelm me when two of the most loving and comforting arms wrapped around me. I couldn't begin to understand or explain the peace I felt in those arms.

"Why are you crying, beautiful?"

Even through the tears and the pain, I knew that voice, I knew those arms. I tried to quiet the sobs as I sat up in the bed turning to him, looking deep into his eyes. I couldn't believe it; he was alive. But how? Jason was so strong. How did he get away and without even a scratch? I quickly searched his face and eyes for any sign of pain or discomfort. I saw none, but still I felt no relief.

"But...how? Why? But..." I tried to convey my questions, but they just seemed to get jumbled in my confusion on the way out of my mouth. My mind was trying to understand that Luke was okay, that he was here in front of me unharmed while my heart was attempting to mourn for a loss it thought was inevitable. I pulled him close, crying into his shoulder.

"Rachel? Are you okay?"

"I don't know...I thought you were going to die. How...?"

"How what? How did I get away? Just a little trick I've picked up," he informed me with the most crooked grin. I wanted to slap him or hug him; I'm not exactly sure which. After a moment's hesitation, I straddled Luke's lap, kissing him passionately. My heart still felt broken, and I needed to know he was there, that he was real. He couldn't have been more than five minutes behind us, but in that short time, I had convinced myself he was going to die. Luke wrapped his arms around me while I poured all my love and concern into that kiss.

"Baby, I love you. Come here," he said, moving me off his lap. He laid me down and held me. I laid there in his embrace, thanking my lucky stars that he hadn't succumbed to the wretched fate I was so sure he was destined to. Times like these is when I really wished I was an optimist, but sadly I was a pessimist. I always assumed the worst until proven wrong.

I softly closed my eyes, and behind my lids, images quickly flashed. I saw my family gathered in the living room just talking. They all seemed so happy. This vision was odd; I was seeing my family but not through my eyes. I was looking through Luke's eyes. I suddenly felt a searing jolt of fear encompass me; it was like nothing I had ever felt before. It felt as though my heart was being ripped from my chest. I knew they weren't my feelings, they were Luke's. In the present realm, I kept my eyes closed as I attentively watched the events unfold in front of me. Luke gave Ryan a look that apparently he understood even if I didn't. I heard as Luke explained quickly to our parents that I was gone. They didn't ask any questions, only simply nodded as Luke and Ryan left the house. Luke ran quickly through the woods with Ryan right on his heels until they found me talking with Jason deep in the woods. He watched, listened, and waited for an opening. When he had it, he stepped into the clearing. Ryan picked me up when Luke ordered him to get me out of there, but this time it was as if I was the one giving the order. The fear swept through me once again as I watched but through Luke's eyes this time. He watched me as I drifted farther and farther away until he could barely make out Ryan's back far off in the distance.

His eyes raced back toward Jason in a rage. I could feel Luke's anger. I could feel every one of his emotions as if they were my own. He was so mad he was shaking. Jason crouched like a tiger on the hunt. Luke paid attention to Jason's every muscle move. In what can only be described as light speed, Jason pounced at Luke in an attack. I couldn't help it as my body tensed, just as Luke's had in preparation for the monster's collision with him. Luke just stood there, tensed awaiting the collision, and then at the very last second, he simply lifted his arm as if to spat the vampire away. I couldn't believe it. This was his masterful plan—to swat him as if he were a lonesome fly. I saw Jason's body being hurled through the air like he was a feather caught in the wind. His body was sent spinning into some poor tree. I watched as the tree split in half and tumbled to the ground on top of his body.

"Are you okay?" Luke asked, pulling me from my vision.

I nodded and hesitantly asked, "How did you do that?"

"Do what?"

I could take the time to explain it to him, but I knew that would cause more questions. Questions I didn't have answers to at the moment. I have always seen the future, but what I just saw I knew without any doubt was the past. It was new and strange and something that I knew I would need to explore more at some point. *Yay, another thing to figure out. Woo-hoo.*

"Nothing, never mind," I told him, shaking my head.

I have never had a vision like the one the other night, but I have never just touched someone and seen what they saw.

Why now? I am stressed enough. I don't need anything else distracting me from the task at hand, I tried to tell myself. *On the other hand, if I have new powers, I should learn to master them, right? Great, now I am arguing with myself. That can never be good.*

Just then, I felt Luke shake underneath me. I turned in his arms to look at him just as he gave me the most innocent look he could muster through his silent laughter.

"Your inner monologue is hilarious…I'm sorry." He quickly shut up and looked like a child that had just told a huge secret that they weren't supposed to tell.

"Excuse me?" I asked once I managed to get my mouth to work again. "And how is it you would know what my inner monologue sounds like exactly?"

"Umm…okay, look, Rachel, I don't want you to be mad."

"Hmm…I don't know. It really depends on how long you've been able to read my mind," I said, sitting up and staring at him.

"Since I met you?" he said, looking away from me in embarrassment.

"What? Since you met me? Are you kidding, 'cause I don't think it's funny."

"No, I'm not joking."

"Really, and you never thought I might want to know that my boyfriend is a mind reader?"

"I'm not," he defended quickly.

"What do you mean you're not? You just said you could hear my thoughts."

"Only yours. That's part of the reason I didn't tell you right away. I had no clue what was going on myself. You know it's very disconcerting having someone else's thoughts in your head."

"Oh really. I bet it's no worse than finding out every thought you've had for the past year wasn't private."

"Look, babe, I'm sorry and I love you. I promise we will talk more about this later, but right now, you need to get some sleep. You've had a long day."

"Really, Luke? Really? You actually think you can drop that bomb on me and then tell me that I need to go to sleep?" I asked, glaring at him. "Can you always hear me?"

"No, not during your visions."

"So just my thoughts, hopes, prayers, and dreams, everything that should only be mine. Damn it, Luke, didn't you think this might be something that I'd want to know?"

"I'm sorry, I can't tell you how many times I started to tell you and nothing came out. I don't know why I can hear your thoughts. At first, I wasn't sure what I was hearing, and when I finally figured it out, I still didn't understand how it was possible. My only thought is that our connection is that strong."

"Great," I huffed, lying back down; arguing wasn't going to stop him from hearing my thoughts so what was the point. "If you could always hear my thoughts, why didn't you tell me what I was? You had to have known what I was going through, what not knowing was doing to me."

"I did...and I wanted to, but I didn't know how to."

"You should've told me," I said in a huff.

"What did you see a while ago?" Luke asked quietly after a few minutes.

"Huh? What do you mean?"

"When we first laid down, everything went silent for a few minutes, then you started arguing with yourself."

"Oh that. I don't know. I saw what happened in the woods but through your eyes. I don't know what it was. It was weird. I've never done anything like that before."

"Okay, how about we get some sleep. We can figure all this out in the morning."

With a sigh, I nodded as he placed a kiss on my forehead. Soon I was snuggled tightly into his loving and caring arms fast asleep. I still couldn't explain how he'd manage to make me feel so comfortable. With him, it felt like for the first time in my life I was able to be someone. He gave me the ability and strength to be someone better than just me. He's such a good person. Why he would want me, I have no idea. I didn't feel good enough for him, but that feeling was what pushed me every day to be better. I felt as though I had barely closed my eyes when I felt the gradual warmth on my skin from the morning's rising sun.

"Good morning, gorgeous," I heard him whisper as he placed a loving kiss on the top of my head.

"Mmm. Good morning," I replied, stretching. "Holy crap. What time is it?" I asked in a rush as I rolled out of bed.

"Almost nine, why?"

"Um, because we have school," I replied, looking at him like he was stupid.

"Uh, yeah, we talked about it last night. We thought it would be best if we all stayed home today since yesterday was a pretty bad day," Luke informed me, looking rather sheepish.

"Great," I mumbled as I stumbled off to take a shower, and Luke headed downstairs to see if there was anything he could do to help with breakfast.

Okay, so I have to get everyone to focus today and work on our strategy. I can't allow them to continue to put this off. Plus if I'm sleepwalking now, there is so much more risk. Great, I told myself once I finished my shower. I had a dream last night. Everything I assumed my family had planned was there in that dream. Granted I couldn't be sure it was their plan seeing as how they wouldn't share anything with me. But still it was there in the dream. They would go into the woods where the clearing was. Far enough away from Clair, mom, and I and from any dense population of people that everyone should be safe. What they didn't know is that Jason, Kaylee, and Brad wouldn't be there. They intended to break off and come for me at the house, where they had so conveniently left me unprotected. Jason would get what he wanted, me, and my family would die. I couldn't allow my family to be destroyed. I knew I had to do something, but I still hadn't figured it all out yet.

"Dad, I think we need to talk about what we are all going to do," I started as we all sat down for breakfast.

"What do you mean 'we,' Rachel? You aren't going to do anything."

Yeah, because I'm just your little girl. Sure, I can't help. It's just so much better for everyone I love to run off and get themselves killed for me or because of me, I thought.

"Dad, I already told you—you know what, never mind. What are all of you going to do? I've been having visions more often lately. I think if I try perhaps I can keep an eye on Jason, watch his moves, see what he is doing and planning."

"No, Rachel, we all want you just to stay here and take it easy for a while, sweetheart. You need to rest and to recoup. You have been through a big ordeal lately, and I want you to recover. Now stop worrying about all of this, and let us do our job," my dad explained with a disgruntled face.

I can't believe this. He really wants me to do nothing, to sit by and wait to be told that I am alone and that it's all because of me. Yeah...okay, well I'm not going to let that happen, I can't. I left everyone in the dining room and went upstairs to Luke's room to plan. I wasn't there long before Luke joined me.

"Hey, can we talk?" he asked as he took a seat on his bed.

Despite my overwhelming want to say no, I knew I couldn't. "Yeah, sure, why not?"

"Rachel, we need to talk about what you are planning, and please don't argue or lie to me by saying that you're not planning anything. It would only insult me."

"Fine," I huffed "What do you want to know? I mean, you should already know everything that I know but—"

"Why?"

"Why? Why what?'

"Why are you doing all of this? Why do you find it necessary to be putting yourself in harm's way like this? I know you're scared of all of us dying, but you do understand that we have been training for this exact thing our whole lives."

"Luke, it's not like that. I just don't want to be here alone and useless. Besides, I have already seen it. Jason knows that all of you would never let me fight. He plans on sending someone after me while the rest keep everyone occupied in battle. So I feel like if they are going to get to me either way, why should I wait here doing nothing when I could be with everyone at least trying to help? I would prefer it to be on my terms."

"Rachel, I can't have you out there. We will all be worried, and none of us will be at the top of our game. Why can't you understand that?"

"Because I don't want to be left alone in the world. I can't lose you. Luke, you are everything to me. I can't lose you," I said shaking my head as my tears dripped onto my hands.

"I know, I know, baby. I can't lose you either, which is why I need you to stay here. I promise I will be okay, that we will all be okay, but I can't do this if I'm worried about you the whole time. Rachel, I love you, and if anything happens to you, it will destroy me," Luke said, pulling me onto his lap.

Seeing that there was going to be no winning this, I simply nodded my understanding and let him hold me for a few minutes before he got up and left. Suddenly I felt as though my life was falling apart. I knew that my dad and Luke loved me; I knew the reason they were doing all this was because they thought they were protecting me. I did understand it, but it didn't mean I had to like it. It didn't mean that I had to listen. *I have never been the ordinary teenager. I don't go out and party, I don't disobey my parents, or at least I never have up until now. How could they ask me to do nothing? How could they expect it? Do they not know me at all anymore? I can't do this. Right now, I have to get out of here.*

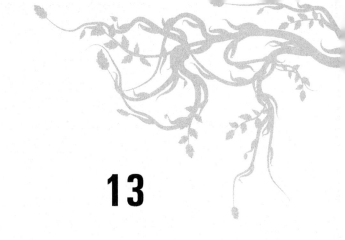

13

Attempting to be as quiet as possible, I made my way to the window, slowly opening it. I looked down at the ground and knew as soon as I did that it was a mistake. I was a story up.

If I fall, I won't die. I might break a bone, but that's it, I tried unsuccessfully to comfort myself. I took a deep breath and threw my legs out the window. *Here we go*, I told myself as I made my descent. I was pretty surprised at myself; I really was turning out to be your regular spider girl. I was almost to the ground when that thought crossed my mind, causing me to chuckle, which in turn caused me to lose my footing, and not being one with much upper body strength, I plummeted to the ground, landing roughly on my bottom. "Ouch," I whimpered. I stood up rubbing my behind as I limped off.

I knew where I was going for the first time since all of this started. I had to talk to someone, someone outside of the family, someone who would hear me out and understand my viewpoints or at least try to understand them. I also knew that I couldn't just tell any old person what we were or what we could do; I had to be careful. So I was headed to the one person who I could always tell anything to, but I knew she was at school and I was going to have to wait for a few hours till she got out. *Probably should've thought of that while I was still in the house.* I sent up a silent prayer that Luke wouldn't come looking for me before I was done. I took my phone out of my pocket and texted Brooke: "911." I didn't need to put anything else. I knew Brooke would find a way to get out of school and meet me at her house.

"Rachel! Oh my god, how are you? Are you okay?" Brooke asked before I could even knock on the door.

"Hey, Brooke…can I come in?"

"Of course. Is everything all right? What's with the 911?"

My eyes started to sting with tears as we made our way upstairs to her bedroom. I knew Brooke would understand, and I knew that she would keep my secret. I mean, she had to after I kept hers for all these years, right?

"Do you remember when you first told me the story of your family?" I had to start small, ease my way into this. She nodded, and I continued, "Okay well, what if I said I found out something even weirder and more crazy about my family?"

I could tell by the look on her face that she was worried it had taken her years to finally accept who she was. Only recently had she actually started to embrace it. "You can tell me anything. I'm here for you, just like you were there for me."

Now what was the easiest way to tell her? "Do you remember the bedtime story my dad told me growing up about the guardians?"

I could tell by her face that it took her a moment to remember, and then I could see it in her eyes when it clicked. "It's all true, isn't it?" she asked. "That's why you can do the things you can."

"Wait, how do you know what I can do?" I asked surprised.

"Rachel, I love you. You are basically my sister, and you suck at lying and hiding things. I don't know exactly what you can do. I know at the cemetery, for Adam's funeral, some things weren't where they should have been. I'm pretty sure it isn't normal for things to hover a few inches off the ground. I know you get headaches with blood running out of your nose, ears, and sometimes your eyes. Now I'm not a doctor, but I'm pretty sure that isn't normal or healthy."

"What happened at the cemetery?" I asked, totally confused by that one. I knew I had made everything levitate in the parking lot, but I was fairly sure no one saw it.

"At the grave site, most of the floral arrangements were about two inches off the ground. I knew how upset you were, and when I took your hand, everything went back to normal, so I assumed it was you."

I couldn't fight the tears anymore; it was so much to take in. I hadn't had the time to accept all of it yet myself, let alone tell anyone else. Now to find out I wasn't as good at hiding it as I thought. I knew Brooke was my lifesaver; at this point, she was more like my life preserver, keeping me afloat. So often recently, I felt as though I was treading water to no uncertain end barely being able to stay afloat. Brooke sat there holding me, whispering soothing words to calm me.

Once the tears had subsided, I continued to explain to her that I was going to need her help. Brooke was a witch in a long line of witches; due to this, she was very powerful. My prayer was that with her help, this war would be won. I was certain that Jason would be unable to see this coming.

We made our way downstairs, and as we were nearing the landing, the door suddenly burst open, and in barged Luke and Ryan. I wasn't even aware of what was going on before Luke had run up the stairs and pulled me into his arms, planting kisses all over my face. Ryan, on the other hand, didn't look too happy; in fact, he was fuming. I could see by the looks on their faces that a lecture was coming.

"What in the hell is wrong with you, Rachel? Do you know what went through our minds when we saw that you were missing? Do you know what you did to everyone, just running off like that?" Ryan immediately started in on me.

"I'm sorry. I didn't realize that I was under lockdown. So that's it, now I'm confined to the house? That's what everyone wants, isn't it?" I yelled out in anger. I was sick of it, sick of the way everyone was treating me. I wasn't a child, and I wasn't helpless. I had powers.

"The hell you didn't know, Rachel. You knew exactly what you were doing, that's why you snuck out. You knew we wouldn't have let you go alone. Do you not get it? They are looking for you! Not us. You, Rachel! They want you!"

"Yeah, I get it Ryan, I do. I understand what it means. I understand that all of you, every last one of you, think you know better than me. That no one will ever trust me like they did Madeline and listen to my advice, and why would they? I'm not her. In everyone's eyes, I am a child, nothing more, nothing less. I could help. I know more that I haven't shared. I have figured things out that no one but me knows, but none of you even wants to listen to me. So it's fine. I'll go back home like the good little girl that I am."

I stormed out of Brooke's house and into Ryan's car. The car ride home was quiet; I had nothing left to say to any of them. I could feel the tears brimming my eyes, but I refused to let them fall, at least until I got home and into my own room. *But we weren't going to my home*, I thought, making me angry. No, my house, my home, was no longer safe. I had no one to talk to and no space that was mine. Everything was being taken away from me; maybe it would be best if I were just gone. I heard Luke suck in a breath at the thought. It was only barely in my head, but I suppose it was enough. I looked up and caught Luke's eyes in the mirror. I could tell he wanted to say something, but I knew he would wait till we were alone.

Once we arrived back at the house, which, thankfully, only took all of ten minutes the way Ryan was driving, I quickly got out of the car and ran into the house. I didn't say a word to anyone. Ignoring their questioning eyes, I headed straight to Luke's room, shutting and locking the door. All my things were in Nathan's, room, but it didn't feel like mine, not that Luke's did, but I felt closer to him than anyone else. I wasn't in the mood for a visitor, not even Luke, which I had to admit was a first. Besides I was pretty sure I already knew what he was going to say. I wanted nothing more than to be alone and wallow in my hate and anger for the moment. I could hear them talking about me downstairs, about what I had said and what they were going to do with me. It sounded like I was a misbehaving child, on drugs, or out partying. I wasn't though, never. I wonder if they have a show for something like this... *Next on supernatural intervention*. No, I just wanted to help my family, a stupid selfless act with so many consequences.

I heard Luke come upstairs and knock on the door. I didn't say anything when he asked if he could come in. I know he sat out there for a while before he finally gave up and went back downstairs. I felt horrible for the way I was acting, which only helped to make me angrier.

At some point, I'm not sure when, but I did eventually cry myself to sleep. It was a fitful sleep with little actual rest. I kept seeing the same things, things that I knew would soon come to pass and things I wanted to stop but knew they wouldn't let me. In my dreams, it always happened the same way: Jason and his minions lure the family from the house, leaving only mom, Clair, and me. At which point Jason, Brad, and Kaylee double back to the house while the guys are fighting tons of vampires, werewolves, and shape-shifters. They are severely outnumbered and don't stand a chance, neither do Clair and my mom in trying to fight off Jason, Brad, and Kaylee. I'm still locked upstairs in a room. In the long run, they all die, and Jason finally gets what he wants: me.

I had to figure it out, and I knew that my grandfather and Brooke were the answer to my problems. Now to just be able to do it without someone intervening. Brooke and I had discussed some of my plans before the boys showed up. However, we didn't get a chance to discuss the finer details. I would have to call her to finish the talk. I suppose I could text her, which would mean no one could over hear our conversation, but with text, if I forgot to delete it and anyone got ahold of my phone, I would be busted. I had figured out a way to block my thoughts from Luke, which was a good start. It was a key element in my plan. If he could hear all my thoughts, my plan would never make it beyond what it is now, a thought. Brooke thought that with concentration, I could keep Luke out of my head for a time at least. It definitely wasn't a long-term fix, but hey, you've gotta work with what you've got.

I could hear everyone awake downstairs, moving around. I didn't eat at all yesterday with everything going on, so I knew that I was going to have to face my judge, jury, and executioner eventually. Reluctantly, I rolled out of bed and got into the shower, thanking my lucky stars that Luke had a bathroom en suite. I took my time; other than a rumbling stomach, I was in no hurry to get downstairs and listen to all the crap they were going to spew. After my shower, I inspected my injuries to see how they were healing. To my surprise, they were all gone. There wasn't a mark on me anywhere. *That's unusual*, I thought. I figured it just to be more of my powers coming through. Everyone other than my family did keep telling me how powerful I was.

As I went to get dressed, I realized my mistake and cursed under my breath. All of my clothes were still in Nathan's room. I wrapped my towel back around me and quickly made my way down the hall, praying the whole way that the room was empty. Thankfully, it was, and I quickly got dressed in a tank top and shorts eager to see what everyone had to say about my healing. Once I was in the dining room where everyone was seated, I plastered on a fake smile and kissed my father's cheek, then went and sat in my usual seat.

"Well, someone seems to be happier today," my father commented.

"And why shouldn't I be happy, Daddy? The sun is shining, I have everyone I love around—oh, and I am being held prisoner in someone else's home. Life is just great," I said, losing my smile and replacing it with an icy stare. I would be a good little girl and do what I was told, but that didn't mean I was going to make it easy on any of them. Okay, that was a total lie. I wasn't going to be a good girl; I was going to do whatever I had to in order to assure everyone I cared about survived this battle.

"Rachel, could we please give it a rest? After everything you've been through, we are just trying to look out for you."

"What is it that I have been through, Daddy? Please tell me since you seem to have all the answers. Do you even know? Look at me. Really look at me. Do I look like I have been through anything. No!" I happily watched their shocked faces scanning my body for the massive amounts of damage that had still been evident the night before.

Clair was the first to ask, "Rachel, what happened? Where are all the bruises and cuts?"

"To be honest, I don't know. I noticed that they were all gone after my shower this morning. But it helps to prove my point that I can help fight. I can help my loved ones. If I am healing faster than normal, I will be safer." I was met with disgruntled faces yet again. *Eh, it's worth a try*, I thought. "Okay, before everyone starts yelling at me again, forget it. Never mind. One day you will all understand what I was saying, and you will regret the way you treated me. I have seen it. Just wait."

I sat and finished my food as the conversation resumed around me, almost as if I had never spoken.

Another day without school at this rate I had no idea how any of us were going to pass. Of course my dad had it all worked out; he had gone to the school and picked up all our missed work for yesterday and today. Apparently he had used his powers to ensure that there would be no consequences to the excessive amount of classes we all had missed. We were to have the missed work complete and ready to turn in the next morning. The boys were going to be training today. Luckily they have known what they were all their lives, so they were better prepared than I was. They would be working on their marksmanship first, followed by who knows what. They were all pretty fluent with a gun and a crossbow since they had been hunting since they were young.

I sat in Luke's room watching out his back window as my dad and Mark gave the boys better instruction. I could hear Clair downstairs with my mom teaching her some intermediate first aid. I sat sourly in the room, angry that it would seem everyone would be allowed to contribute something to this battle except me. They were even letting Clair help, and she was just human.

I would be helping though, just not in the formal way, not in the way I wanted. I wanted to be accepted and understood at least by my own family. If they couldn't accept me and understand me, what chance did I have with the rest of the world? My dad used to understand me; he used to care about my visions and what I saw. Now it just seemed like everyone was trying to shut me out. Then again, maybe they have always been trying to shut me out. I mean they never told me what I was or what I was capable of.

I shut the blinds on the window and got up, I needed to be doing something, anything besides just sitting here and thinking about what could have been or what things could be like. Thanks to my visions, I realized probably better than anyone how short life truly can be, and I didn't want to have regrets. If I were to die tomorrow, I wanted to know that I had lived my life to the best of my ability. However after learning what I was and at least to some degree what I was capable of, I had a lot of regrets, what ifs, and could haves. I shook my head, trying to clear it of those thoughts; I knew they wouldn't do me any good. I needed to start taking action and preparing for what I was going to do whether they liked it or not.

I figured being in better shape would help in the long run. I knew my endurance wasn't what it should be or could be for that matter. Since I had stopped cheerleading, to be honest, my endurance had certainly gone down. I went to the gym in the basement as quietly as possible. I didn't want to draw attention to myself. I had said my piece on the matter, and so had they, and I wasn't in the mood to hear it anymore. What good would it do anyway? I wasn't willing to budge on the matter, and neither were they. I would be in this fight whether they liked it or not. I ran on the treadmill while listening to my iPod for as long as I could. When I couldn't take it anymore and felt like my lungs were going to burst, I looked down and was surprised to see that I had actually pushed myself to run ten miles. Not bad, I guess. I could have done worse. I wasn't done in here though. I need strength and endurance, so I moved on to the weights starting at five pounds and working my way up slowly. By the end of it, I was able to do fifteen reps with the twenty-pound weights, but I was drenched in sweat, dog tired, and moving my arms was really painful. So I decided to give it a rest for today and went back to Luke's room to shower. I guess I should be thankful no one was griping about that at least.

I wasn't as sneaky on my way out of the gym because I got tons of curious and suspicious looks, but I ignored them and continued heading for his room. If they were going to keep me in this house, there was no way I was going to let them tell me what I could and couldn't do while here. After a quick shower and an even quicker dinner, I quickly did the makeup work for school that I had missed. I was so thankful for being a person that doesn't really have to study. I managed to finish it all in two hours.

I missed my room and my things; I missed having my own space. I felt like an outsider here, and with the way everyone was treating me, it just made that feeling all the stronger. I could've been living in a house full of strangers and felt more at home than my family was making me feel as of late.

———— ◆ ————

School was more frantic now that it was the last few months before summer break, and all the teachers were trying to fit the rest of their lessons in. I had much bigger problems to think about than passing, so I couldn't say that I paid much attention. Granted there was a part of me that wasn't sure I would live to see my senior year anyways, so what did it all matter. Lunch was spent with Brooke, and I brainstorming about what we could do to stop this battle. I knew no matter what Jason wasn't going to stop until he got me. We had gone over everything we could think of—spells, fighting, running away, hiding, everything. I had to admit I was blessed to have such a good friend. Not only did she believe me but was willing to try and help me; I can't imagine many others who would have been willing to do the same. Finally after about a month of not coming up with anything useful, Brooke finally had an idea.

"Okay, so here is what we are going to do. First, I think I should start by doing a blocking spell. This way Luke can't get into your head. That should take some stress off you. Then we should do a protection spell on your houses so that nothing intending any of you harm can enter. This way you don't have to worry about that vision as much. I'm not saying that they couldn't find a way around it, but it should make it harder for them. And I was thinking…well, I don't know, my last idea is kind of crazy."

"Brooke, just tell me. I'm willing to do anything. You know that."

"Okay, so I was thinking I could also do a linking spell."

"A linking spell? What's that?"

"Well, essentially what I'll be doing is linking everyone's lifeline to yours, which would be great, seeing as how they want to take you alive. So pretty much as long as your alive, no one linked to you will die."

"That's great, Brooke, you're a genius."

"Well, not really. See, here's the thing, all magic has loopholes. You see, if all the people you were linked to happened to die at the same time or before the spell brought them back, it would possibly, most likely, could kill you as well."

"Wow, oh my god, you are brilliant. That's perfect!"

"Huh?"

"Well, you see, if I succeed in keeping them alive, they will eventually win. I mean, no one can fight forever, right? And if I don't, then I die, and Jason still doesn't get what he wants. It's the perfect plan."

"Okay. Right, I guess if you look at it like that, then yeah, it's perfect. But, Rachel, you do realize what you're saying, right?"

"Yup."

Brooke simply nodded. Being my best friend, she knew better than anyone not to try and argue with me once I had something in my head. "Okay, I'll try to get out of the house tomorrow. Will you be ready to do the spells by then?"

"Yeah. I mean, I should be." And with that we headed to our classes.

Once at home in the evenings, I mostly spent the time watching the boys train through one of the bedroom windows. I felt sorry for them in a way, even if I never would tell them. On top of all the homework, they now had two hours of weapons practice to deal with. Dad and Mark were training them to use all sorts of weapons. They had a bow that shot stakes, handguns, rifles, shotguns, machine guns, silver bullets, wooden bullets. They also had knives, stakes, crosses, ultraviolet flash bangs, hand grenades that when exploded shot out wood splinters, silver, and CO_2 charged cartridges that expelled holy water. It was scary even thinking about what was to come. I often wondered whether our troops got this kind of training before heading into war.

However, with all the training, it didn't leave much time for anything else. Luke and I rarely got moments alone with each other, and when we did, there was barely time for a stolen kiss, much less actual talking. Not that I minded much. I really didn't have anything to say to him as long as he was going to continue to be stubborn and not listen to me. I didn't have the energy to fight with any of them anymore. Plus, being mad at Luke hurt deep in my soul. I never wanted to be mad at him. I knew what was to come had the power to make us or break us, and that was terrifying. I tried my best to put on my big girl panties and do what I had to.

If I was honest, all I really wanted to do was go running to my daddy. I wanted him to tell me that the monster didn't exist. I wanted him to scare the bogeyman away just like he used to when I was little. That's what daddies are there for after all.

14

Saturday morning, I got up with a plan in my head, and I was determined to follow through with it despite how bad I was sure I was going to feel afterward. I spent the day wallowing around in Luke's room or down in their gym. Finally around three o'clock, I went back upstairs to take a shower. I was very sore now that time had passed, and I had been pushing my body for the last month; the only thing I wanted was a good nap. However, I still wasn't done, and sleep could wait because I knew once Jason had his plan in motion, he wouldn't wait for me. So I turned on some quiet music, lit some candles, and sat in the middle of Luke's floor, and tried to meditate. It was something I had never really done before, but Brooke had recommended that it might help since it helps her before she performs some of her more complex spells. So there I sat, trying to clear my mind, which is much harder than one might think. I guess I did eventually achieve my meditative state because the next thing I knew, Luke was knocking on his door, telling me that I missed lunch and dinner was almost ready. I felt almost sorry that I had kicked him out of his room for the most part, but I tried not to dwell on that thought.

I should get up and go down there, I should talk to them, and I should forgive them. I know they are only trying to protect me, to save me. I understood that they were doing all of this out of nothing other than the love they all shared for me. Nonetheless, if I could recognize them and their side, why won't they take the time to understand and see my side or, at the very least, try to. With a sigh, I stood up, blew out my candles, and headed downstairs.

I didn't say anything to anyone as I took my usual seat. Everyone was watching me, staring at me, waiting for my next meltdown. I rolled my eyes and continued eating. I was so sick of all of them treating me like some misbehaving child.

"If everyone is just going to sit here and stare at me, I'll go back to the room," I told everyone seriously. I was tired of being treated like a zoo exhibit. I was starting to feel like there should be a sign saying, "Please do not feed or pet the animal."

Still no one said anything. "Fine," I huffed, standing up to leave.

"Rachel, wait, don't go," my dad called out.

"Why shouldn't I? I'm apparently not wanted here. I'm not some zoo animal."

"Oh, Rachel, don't be ridiculous. No one thinks you are a zoo animal," my mom said, rolling her eyes.

"No? Really, Mom? Now after everything, you finally have something to say? Okay then, let's talk. I mean really talk."

"Sure, sweetie. Sit, let's talk. What's on your mind?"

"Hmm. Let's see. Let's start with a general question to everyone. Do you know who Annette is?" Everyone looked at me blankly. I laughed. I think I had finally snapped. "Didn't think so. Okay, Mom, let's try a different question. Do you know what your mother's name was?" I sat there with a smug look on my face as the wheels in my mother's head started to spin. She knew the name; she just didn't know how I did. My mom never really spoke of her mother. She had never told me her name. The only information she had ever shared with me was that her mother died while giving birth to her. "Do you know what she was?"

"Rachel, what are you going on about now? Yes, I know my mother's name. It was Annette, but what does that have to do with anything?"

I was making her angry, I could tell. In my seventeen years, I had done it quite often. She didn't know where any of this was going, and it was upsetting her. "Dad and Mark were the first to have children with humans. Well, technically speaking, Dad didn't have a child with a human."

"What are you talking about, Rachel? I have no powers. I am human."

"No, Mom, you're not, and I think you know that. Annette was a guardian, and Grandpa was a great Indian warrior who could communicate with all things dead and living. So, no, Mom, I wouldn't say that you are human exactly."

Everyone was staring again slack-jawed as if I grew a second head.

"I tried to tell you that I could help, that I was having vision, but for once, Dad, you didn't care to ask. I am going through some of the quickest changes I have ever gone through, and I needed you, but you didn't care to be there for me."

"Sweetie, I never intended to make you feel that way," my dad said, but I couldn't control my temper with them any longer.

"Dad, stop. Just stop. That is exactly the way you wanted me to feel," I said, slamming my fists down on the table and standing up. As I did, the lights started to flicker and the dishes on the table began to rattle. "You spent my whole childhood telling me that one day I would understand my powers and that they would be great, and when that day finally came you weren't there for me. No, when that day came all of you turned your backs on me. You want to lock me away to hide me." As my anger grew so did, the noise, and everything in the house was starting to shake. "So go fight your fight. I will have nothing to do with it as you wish."

The panic on their faces was something I had never seen before. They were all scared; they were scared of me. "So go run off and save the world, but all of you will die trying. I've seen it over and over and over again. I have seen it. You. Will. All. Die."

By the time I finished my rant, my family was hovering in their chairs about three feet off the ground. I didn't know how I did it, but as I calmed down, they all fell. I quickly ran back to Luke's room, slamming the door behind me. I had done what I set out to do. I had made them see my powers and some of my point—at least that's what I hoped I had done. Now the rest was up to them. I knew it wouldn't take my dad long before he followed me up. There was a knock on the door.

"Come in," I yelled.

I was surprised that it was my mother on the other side of the door. My mom and I never really had that close of a relationship; I was always closer to my dad. Some said it was because I was too much like my mom, so we butted heads. But in the midst of my breakdown, there she was. She quietly came into the room and sat down beside me on the bed. She didn't say a word as she reached and just held me in a loving mother's embrace.

"I'm sorry, sweetie. I love you so much, and I am sorry. We never...I never wanted this life for you. I have known all along what I am, but I rejected it at a young age. I don't even know how to access any of the gifts if I tried now. I never wanted this life, and I never wanted it for you. I love you. You're my only child. I wanted to protect you. I wanted to hide you away so that no one could ever find you. I would like to think that I have, for the most part, or as well as we could. Granted it appears all our efforts were for not, 'cause here you are in the thick of things. Do you know that's why we live in this tiny town? I would love to live in the city with all the hustle and bustle, but I felt you would be safer in a place like this. I guess in the end, it was all foolish thinking. I should have know it didn't matter if we tried to hide what you are, that one day it would all catch up to us anyways. I will lay down my life to protect you as will everyone in this house. You are our concern, our love, our life. You are what matters. Let us do this. Let us do what is right."

By that point, I was a crying mess. I could understand where she was coming from better than most. I have the strongest love for my family and friends; it's not something I take lightly at all. But I didn't know how to make her understand that the sacrifices that she and everyone else were willing to make meant nothing. There had to be a way to project my vision on to her. I had to make her see what I saw so that she can understand. I was going to do what I had to do despite what anyone else wanted or said, but it would be easier with my mother on my side, with anyone on my side. I focused all of my energy into our hug and let the outside world go. I tried to push everything I had been seeing into her mind. I wanted to give her a glimpse into the hell that I saw coming for us. I wasn't sure it was working especially when my mother hadn't said anything or moved for almost five minutes. I was about to give up and move away from her when I felt a tear hit my arm. I looked up to see that my mom was just staring at me, crying.

"Okay, sweetie, I'll help you. I'm sorry that things are the way they are. You just have to trust me and believe that everyone downstairs is doing what they honestly think is best for you."

"I know that, Mom. I've never really doubted that. I just wish they would listen to me. They are treating me like I'm a toddler. I need to get to Brooke's house. Can you help me?"

"I can try, sweetie, but you have to be careful. Give me five minutes, then go out the window," she said, standing up and walking out of the room. Just as the door was shutting, she stopped and turned around. "Rachel, try not to break your leg on the way down."

"Yeah, sure, Mom. Jinx me."

Once she was gone, I waited and then headed to the window. I decided to leave my phone at home this time. I didn't need anyone tracking me. As quietly and quickly as I could, I made my way out the window and down the side of the house. Once my feet were firmly on the ground, I took a small sigh of relief. One hard part down, fifty million to go. I quietly took off into the woods, opting to take the trail that would lead close to Brooke's house. I didn't want to take the road and be out in the open this time. In hindsight, taking the woods probably wasn't the best of ideas; it's not like I have had the best of luck in these woods lately. It would take longer, but this way, I wasn't out in the open where everyone could see me and find me as quickly. I wasn't naive. I also knew by going into the woods alone I was putting myself in more danger, but it wasn't my fault they had made it so that I couldn't tell them anything. Twenty minutes later, I was at Brooke's house.

"Good, you made it." She had gotten to the door and opened it before I could even knock.

"Yeah, Mom helped."

"So she is on our side now?"

"I don't know. At this point, I'm not sure what I know anymore."

"It's all going to be okay, Rach. We can do this. I'm going to put a protection spell on both houses and everyone in it, and then I am going to do the linking spell, but first, I'm going to block your mind. I don't have enough strength on my own to do all these, so I need you to lie down. I'm going to pull energy from you to be able to complete the spells. Okay?"

"Yeah, I guess whatever you have to do to keep them safe. Will it hurt?"

"Well…mmm…it uh shouldn't. Itjustmightkillyou." She rushed the last part out so fast I had no idea what she said.

"What was that last bit?"

"Argh. It might kill you. Or me. I'm not sure. I have never done anything nearly this complicated before. I have no way of knowing what it might do to us. I know that the spells I will be casting tonight are not easy, and they need a lot of concentration, strength, and energy. I am hoping with all your ultracool breeding, it will be enough."

"Wow. Way to make me sound like a dog. Okay then. What do you need me to do?"

"Just lie down and relax. I'll do the rest."

As I lie down on the floor in the center of the candles she had set up, Brooke grabbed a book and lit the candles. Soon she sat beside me on the floor.

"You ready?" I nodded. "Okay, first I am going to start with a spell to link us so that I can draw from you. Then we will do the blocking, followed by protection, and finally the linking spell."

Brooke laid her hands gently on me and started chanting in some language that I thought might be Latin. "Quid mihi opus est ut nos accipere pagina. Virtutes invoco solis terrae mihi liceat uti wisi. Quid mihi opus est ut nos accipere pagina. Virtutes invoco solis terrae iungi uti mihi liceat." She kept repeating and rocking; it was very odd and scary to see. Suddenly the flames on the candles shot up, and Brooke stopped chanting.

"Okay, how do you feel?"

"Uh…so far, so good, I guess."

"Good. I'm going to do the blocking spell now, and I will be actually drawing from you. Rachel, once it is started, you cannot stop me no matter what." When I nodded, she started chanting again, something different this time. "Clausus ab animo volenti penetrent. Custodi illam, ut occulta consilia agi. Clausus ab animo volenti penetrent. Custodi illam, ut occulta consilia agi." About halfway through the spell, I started to feel it. It wasn't painful; in fact, it didn't hurt at all. I just suddenly felt very sleepy. Again, when the flames went up, she stopped.

"It's done. Your mind is a vault once again." She looked down at me. "Oh my god. Are you okay?"

"Yeah, I'm fine. What's wrong with you?"

"Your nose...it's bleeding."

Without any thought, I reached up, touching under my nose and feeling the stickiness of blood.

"I'm fine, Brooke, okay? We have to finish this. We have to do the last two spells."

"Okay." She sighed. "This one is going to take more than the last one. Just relax. I'm going to do the protection spell on the houses now." With a deep breath, I closed my eyes and tried my best to relax.

"Pueri servate domum, qui vult eripere eos nocere. Ah, exaudi orationem meam, istum puerum tuum in locum suum. Pueri servate domum, qui vult eripere eos nocere. Ah, exaudi orationem meam, istum puerum tuum in locum suum."

Again the candles shot up, and the chanting ended. I can't quite describe the look on Brooke's face. I think it was somewhere between being proud of the accomplishments of completing her spells and terror.

"Oh my god, Rachel." There were tears in her eyes as she looked at me. I had felt a little pain, but I was mostly tired. I didn't understand the look on her face. "Can you sit up?"

"Of course, what's wrong with you?"

"You have blood dripping from your eyes, ears, and nose. Can't you feel it?"

"What are you talking about?" I asked struggling to sit up. I suppose the spell had taken more out of me than I realized. Brooke handed me a mirror. Looking into it, I saw that she was right. It looked as though I had tears of blood coming from my eyes; it was one of the creepier sights I have ever seen.

"Rachel, I can't do the last spell. It's going to take the most from you, and I'm terrified that it will kill you. I can't kill you. You are my best friend."

Quickly grabbing Brooke's hand, I looked into her eyes, hoping she would understand why she had to finish this. "Brooke, it's my family. You have to finish this. Please, I can't… If anything were to happen to them… I can't… I just can't."

"Okay…okay, lie back," she said, getting the book to the right spell, and whispered, "God, help us."

Once I was in the position, and she had the book in the proper place, the chanting started again. "Accipere in populum, et vincula eorum lifelines amet. Miscere vite gaudet. Aut omnino non commorientibus. Iungente patrocinari. Lorem quos amat. Accipere in populum, et vincula eorum lifelines amet. Miscere vite gaudet. Aut omnino non commorientibus. Iungente patrocinari. Lorem quos amat."

That was all I heard before everything went dark. What I thought to be moments later, I slowly started to open my eyes. I was confused to see Brooke essentially in a ball on top of me, crying, and all the candles and stuff put away. I realized I must have been asleep longer than I thought, but I didn't see why that called for lying on top of me.

"Hey, Brooke, babe, it's kind of hard to breathe down here."

Her first response was to scream and to jump halfway across the room.

"But... How... You were..."

"I was what?" I asked confused and a little sore.

"Rachel you...you were dead. I'm talking cold body, blue lips...the whole nine yards. *You were dead.*"

"Dead? Wow, really? But then, how am I alive? you must have been mistaken."

"I don't know how you are alive and breathing, Rachel, but what I do know is about fifteen minutes ago, you were dead."

"Oh well, it worked, and I'm fine. Nothing to worry about, right?"

"Wrong," came an angry voice from behind me, a voice that every child knows all too well. It was my dad, and he was livid. *Crap!*

"Dad, I can—"

"Stop. What the hell were you thinking? Better question—what the hell were you doing?"

"Nothing, Dad, we were just playing around. Brooke got a spell kit a while back as a joke, and we were just playing around with it, goofing off."

"Get up and get home now. We will talk about this there," my dad said. I could tell by the tone of his voice I was in deep trouble. I guess I could understand, but I was just doing what I felt needed to be done. I just hope he understood that. I hope they all could.

The car ride was eerie silent. I was scared to even breathe. I could feel, see, and sense the anger radiating off my dad. I have no clue how he found me or how much he heard, but I could assume he heard enough to deduce that Brooke thought I was dead. Not five minutes later, we pulled into our driveway. *Thank God.* I'm not sure how much longer I could take sitting in a little car with him.

"Get out, get inside, and don't even think about going to your room. Rachel, we are going to discuss whatever it is that you think you and Brooke were doing."

"We're back at home?" I asked looking around puzzled, by the look on his face I knew he wasn't going to answer. "Dad, just listen to me. I can explain."

"Inside now, Rachel."

I don't think I had ever seen my dad this angry before. For the first time in my life, I was actually scared of him. Quietly, I got out of the car and went inside. Inside the house, everyone was there waiting for me. I could tell by the looks on their faces that no one was happy with what quick glance I gave them. With a huff, I went and sat down on the couch in the living room, not making eye contact with any of them. To be honest, I didn't really care what any of them had to say. I knew what I did was for the best. Soon enough, my dad had entered the room and immediately started in.

"What the hell were you doing, Rachel? What were you thinking? Do you not understand that there are evil demented killers after you?"

I didn't say anything. I had nothing to say to them that I hadn't already tried to say at one point or another. How would I respond even if I did? Sorry, Dad, I was attempting to protect all of you, and in doing so, I might have temporarily gotten myself killed, maybe. *Yup, that about sums up the way the last thing I would ever have gotten to say in this house would go.*

"Well, young lady, do you have nothing to say for yourself?" By the look on my face, my dad continued his rampage. "Damn it, Rachel, say something. Tell me I misunderstood when I heard Brooke say that you had been dead. Tell me it was a joke. Tell me something."

The word *dead* seemed to have gotten everyone's attention. *Yay, here comes the screams and shouts from everyone else. Just what I was looking forward to*, I thought sarcastically.

"Dead?" my mom questioned, holding her chest.

"Come on, Mom. Clearly if I were dead, I wouldn't be here right now getting my head chewed off by Dad now, would I?" I asked, speaking for the first time. I wasn't in the mood for this crap. I simply wanted to go upstairs to bed. I still had no energy. Luke was looking at me like I was some strange puzzle he had never seen.

"Why can't I hear your thoughts?" he finally asked.

"Hmm. Can't you? How odd. May I go to bed now?" I asked, turning back to my father.

"Bed? Really, Rachel? No, no, you can't go to bed until you start explaining yourself."

With a deep breath, I finally just gave in. I was too tired to fight anymore. "Fine, Dad. Let's see… Brooke is a witch, she cast a spell, and I died. Do you have any more questions for me, or can I go to bed now?"

"Really, Rachel? A witch and spells? That's the garbage that you're going to spew to me?"

Well, if I had known he wasn't even going to try to believe me, I would have told him the truth sooner. "Wow, I can't believe someone who knows there are werewolves, vampires, shape-shifters, and God knows what else is out there has a hard time believing in witches. I mean come on, how narrow-minded can you be?" I'm not sure I had meant to say that out loud; however, looking at everyone's faces, now I realize it was definitely a bad idea.

"I don't care if Brooke was a Greek god. Explain to me the dying part. Tell me, Rachel, what did the two of you think you were doing? What spell?"

"Well, no one wanted to listen to me or let me help, so I went to someone who could help me. Brooke's ancestry dates back to Salem. She knows what she's doing, and yes, I knew going into it that there was a chance it could kill me. Granted I was banking on the idea that the supercool quick healing thing would kick in, yay I was right," I said, raising my hands over my head in a kind of cheer motion.

"Forgive me if I don't find the humor in any of this. Okay, well, since we can't trust you to stay in the house and we can't trust you with your friends, here's what we are going to do. Thankfully your mother has her teaching degree because as of today you will no longer be attending school. Your windows will be nailed shut since you like going out of them so much. Oh, and I want your cell phone, computer, and car keys."

I didn't move. I didn't say anything. He had to be joking, right? This was all some bad joke. *Hey, maybe I was still unconscious at Brooke's house, and this was just some screwed-up dream.* Quickly I reached up and pinched my arm.

"Ouch."

"What in the hell are you doing now?" my dad asked.

"I pinched myself."

"Well, I saw that. Why did you pinch yourself?"

"Because there is no way any of this can be real. There is no way that my father just banned me from leaving this house or communicating with anyone outside of this house. I am not some criminal that you can lock away. This isn't some Disney movie. I'm your daughter. You can't treat me like this. What's next? Are you going to lock me in a tower? Better be sure to get rid of all the spinning wheels while you're at it."

"Oh, I think you'll find that I can, and I think I just did, and as far as Disney, you're right because there's no such thing as happily ever after."

"Wow. Really, Dad. So answer me this: what makes you better than Jason then?"

"Go to your room. *Now!*"

"Fine!" I screamed back as the entire house shook, and I stormed up the stairs to my room and slammed the door.

15

've had it with them! They can't treat me like this. They have no right to keep me prisoner in this house. Before my dad had a chance to take my phone, I sent a quick text to Brooke telling her what was going on. I was too angry to sleep, but there wasn't anything else to do either. I had stormed around my room for about an hour before I decided to meditate. As I went to get my candles, I finally stopped to notice that all the furniture in my room had now levitated to my ceiling. As I calmed down, it all came crashing down. Of course, the noise caused everyone downstairs to come running up. They probably thought I had tried to escape again.

"Rachel, are you okay?" my mom asked, being the first to make it into my room.

"Yeah, Mom, I'm fine."

"What happened up here?" she asked, looking around my room.

"I don't know. I was mad and pacing, and then I decided to meditate, and everything just kind of came crashing down."

"Okay, you have made things move a lot lately. Do you want to explain how you're doing it to the rest of us?" my dad asked.

Clearly he was still in a bad mood. *Yay.* "I don't know!" I yelled, causing everything in my room to go flying toward my dad.

"Rachel, stop this!" my mom yelled.

"I can't, I don't know how I'm doing it. I've been able to move small things for a while now if I really concentrated on them, but I don't know how I'm doing any of this. I just get really angry…usually at dad…and stuff just starts moving."

"Why didn't you ever tell me you could do this?" my dad asked, sounding shocked.

"Why would I? Look at the way you've been treating me lately. Why would I tell you anything?"

"Because I'm your father, and I have a right to know."

I couldn't stop myself from laughing. "Just because you're my father doesn't give you a right to know anything. It makes you want to know everything, but wanting and having a right are two very different things. There are so many things you have no clue about me. Dad, you used to be my best friend, but then I grew up, and it just wasn't the same anymore. I couldn't come to you with my problems."

"Rachel, you can always come to me with anything," my dad said, looking regretful for the first time tonight.

"No, I couldn't, Daddy. You wouldn't have known what to do if I would've come to you, and that's okay, but you didn't come to me either. So don't expect it to just go back to the way it was because you want it to. I didn't ask for any of this. I don't want to be this way. I was happy being normal. Granted when I thought I was normal, I had a crappy boyfriend, but that didn't matter. For the most part, I was happy."

"And now?" Luke asked, even though we both knew he didn't need to. Even if he couldn't read my thoughts, he knew me well enough to read my body language.

"Now...now, I've given up. I don't care what happens to me. With the way everyone I love so much treats me, it doesn't matter. Jason can be no worse than all of you have been to me," I said as the tears I had been trying to hold back for so long finally started to fall. I could feel the burning tracks as they raced down my cheeks.

"I'm sorry, Rachel," my dad said. He hung his head and walked out of my room. He truly looked like a broken man. I didn't mean to make him feel that way, but I couldn't take it anymore. I felt utterly alone, and it was suffocating. Even if I was surrounded by people who loved me, I still had the feeling of screaming at the top of my lungs and no one being able to hear me. I just simply couldn't shake it.

Everyone was still in my room staring at me; I knew they wanted to say something, but no one made a move. "It's fine. I'm learning to adjust," I said through tears. My mom stepped forward with her hand held out to comfort me, I think. I merely shook my head stepping away. I didn't want to be comforted and told everything would be okay when I knew it wouldn't be.

"It's fine. I'll talk to her," Luke said, shooing everyone else away.

Once everyone else was gone, I didn't give Luke a chance to say anything. There was nothing he was going to say that was going to make me feel any better. What I needed now was his touch. I needed to feel something. I walked up to him and grabbed his shirt, pulling his body against mine.

"Rachel." It was a ghost of a whisper on my lips as I captured his with mine.

I have no idea how long we stood there kissing, but I poured everything into that kiss. All my anger, love, fear, hate, and longing to be close to him. When I finally pulled away, we were both panting, and his usually blue eyes were so much darker. I could see my lust reflected back in his. Without a thought, I pushed him to the bed with me straddling his lap. Somewhere in the back of my mind, I knew this wasn't going to make me feel any better, but right now I needed it. I needed to feel loved. Feeling the same need I did, Luke grabbed my hips, pulling me down, so there wasn't even enough room for air between us. I sat there for the longest moment staring into those perfect eyes.

"Luke…I love you," I whispered and crashed my lips back to his. We were all rough kisses and groping hands. I ran my hands under his shirt, feeling the muscles of his back and abdomen, sending little shivers through both of our bodies. I don't know how long we sat there kissing. It could have been minutes or years; all I know is I wasn't ready for it to end when he pulled away from me.

"Rachel, I love you too, but this isn't going to make you feel any better. We need to talk," he said in a husky voice.

"I know. But right now all I need is to feel loved, and you make me feel loved," I said in a shaky voice.

I knew the moment was gone; I could still see his lust for me in his eyes, but he was regaining his focus quicker than I would have liked.

"Talk to me," he begged.

"I feel alone even when surrounded by people. I still feel so alone." Taking a deep breath, I cleared my mind, pushing all the visions of their deaths at him. I needed him to see to understand. If no one else would, Luke had to.

After a few moments, he grabbed my hips, roughly pulling me back to him, and crashed his lips back on mine. "I'm sorry you have to see all this," he whispered between kisses. "I won't let go of you. I won't let anyone take you away from me."

"I know, but that's not what scares me. I'm scared they are going to take you away from me. Luke, I can't lose you… not you," I said through tears and soft kisses. The passion was still there in our touches and kisses, but this wasn't about that anymore; this was about love and reassurance and the fear of loss. I think we both needed this connection.

With a simple roll of his hips, Luke had moved us so that I was lying on the bed with him on top of me. I could feel his weight pushing me down into the mattress; it was a delicious feeling of being surrounded by him. His lips were at the base of my throat, kissing, licking, sucking, making my body feel like it was going to explode in fireworks. I ran my hands under his shirt, feeling the muscles in his back moving under the skin as he continued to tease my body with his mouth. Before I knew what I was doing, I had his shirt off and thrown across the room. He really was wearing too many clothes, I thought. Breaking the contact his lips had with my skin, he quickly removed my shirt adding it to the floor.

"Luke, I need you," I whispered into his ear, causing him to shiver.

"We shouldn't" was his only response as he kissed me from my shoulder to my neck.

With my legs wrapped around his waist, I pulled him closer to me, grinding us together. "I don't care," I groaned.

Unfortunately, that was as far as it got because at that very moment, Nathan walked in, staring openmouthed and, I think, a little frightened. "Crap," I said, sitting up and pushing Luke to the other side of the bed.

"Great timing," Luke said, standing to grab our shirts off the floor.

"I'm sorry… I should—I'm sorry," Nathan stumbled, turning around to leave.

"No, it's fine. What's up?" Luke said, throwing me my shirt and pulling his over his head.

"You know, if you are going to do the deed, you could at least lock the door," Nathan informed us.

"Did you need something?" Luke asked, looking more irritated than I had ever seen him.

"I just wanted to make sure Rachel was okay," Nathan said, looking sheepish.

"Aww. I'm fine. I'm sorry I exploded on everyone earlier," I said, finally getting off the bed.

"Okay." Nathan nodded and left, closing the door behind him.

"Well, that was crappy timing," I mumbled, turning to face Luke.

"Yeah. I'm going to go downstairs and talk with everyone or take a cold shower. Maybe your dad is calmer now."

"Good luck with that. I'm going to bed," I told him as he left the room.

Once he was gone, I changed into my pajamas and went to bed. I can't say I was happy to be alone again, but I had a lot to think about, and it was easier to think when I was alone.

I wasn't sure how I won the argument with my dad, and to be honest, it didn't feel much like a victory. I hated seeing my dad like that; I never wanted to hurt him. I just wanted him to see me. Not his little girl, but the strong woman I was becoming.

I sat down in the middle of my floor and, using my mind, slowly started to put my room back together. When everything was finally back in its place, I went to my bed and lay down. I was too tired to care about anything else tonight.

The morning sun kissed my skin, and slowly I rolled over snuggling into Luke's chest. He was so warm and comforting. But it didn't feel right. I remember going to sleep, but Luke wasn't there. Slowly I opened my eyes to see Adam with his arms wrapped tightly around me.

"No!" I screamed, jumping away as fast as I could. It wasn't possible; he was dead.

"It's okay, Rach. I'm not here to hurt you."

"Great. What do you want?" I asked, still incredibly scared at seeing my dead ex in my bed.

"To warn you. They are all going to die," Adam said without any feeling in his voice.

"No, they won't, not if I have anything to say about it. I will give up my own life first," I told him. Even I could hear the despair in my voice.

"Rachel, I am sorry about the last few months before I died. For what it's worth, I did love you," he told me as he placed a whisper of a kiss on the top of my head.

"Thanks, Adam," I whispered as I watched him fade into nothing, like a memory. I couldn't believe what I just heard and was kind of shocked that no one came to check on me after I screamed. In fact, I could hear nothing from everyone else. *They must still be sleeping*, I thought as I quietly made my way out of bed and downstairs.

The house was eerily silent, and a sense of dread fell over me as I rushed down the stairs, trying to be careful not to trip. Something wasn't right. Picking up my pace, I ran into the living room. What I saw made me stop dead in my tracks. There was blood everywhere; it was dripping off the walls. It was like something out of a movie, but I saw no bodies. It wasn't possible that I slept through something like this. It was a massacre. Where were the bodies? Where was my family?

I checked the whole house quickly and still found no one. I found more blood but no bodies. This can't be happening. I tried to calm down and slow my pounding heart, but nothing seemed to help. Where was my family? Running outside, I started to scream. "Mom! Dad!" I frantically searched for a sign of anyone. "Luke!"

After I searched the house and yard about a thousand times, I finally gave up. I wasn't going to find them here. I sat down on the steps in front of our house and started to cry. I was too late. They were all dead, and I couldn't save them. Worse than that, I slept through it and didn't even tell them how much they meant to me. I'll never get to tell them that I love them again or give them one more hug or hear their laughs. What was I going to do? "No, Luke, you promised me. You promised this wouldn't happen. Where are you?" I sobbed.

"Rachel? Rachel? Come on, sweetie. You have to wake up." I could hear my dad's voice, but it didn't make any sense. I was awake.

"Dad! Dad! Where are you? Please help me. I don't want to be alone. Daddy, please!" I cried.

I just wanted to be back in the arms of my parents. "Please!" I pleaded with no one and everyone. I cried for what felt like forever. I could still hear my father's voice begging me to come back, but it didn't make any sense. Where was I supposed to come back to? When I managed to get my crying under control, I opened my eyes to see my family and loved ones standing around my bed. My dad was sitting next to me on my bed. He had practically dragged me into his lap. It was all a dream. It was all a dream.

"Oh my god, baby, are you okay?" my dad asked when he saw my eyes open.

"No, Daddy, no, I'm not okay. You were all dead," I cried into my father's chest. "You were all dead."

"Shush, shush. It's okay, sweetie, we are all here. We're going to be fine, honey. It's all right."

Little by little, I managed to stop crying and was able to regain some control over my breathing. Looking up from my hole that I had made in my dad's arms, I could see the concerned faces of my family. I felt sorry for them; I can tell by the looks on their faces they are at a loss on how to help me. Hell, I don't even know how to help me anymore.

"All right. Who's going to help with breakfast?" my mother asked. Leave it to her to be the one to break this awkward silence we had going. Leaving Luke and me alone, everyone followed my mom downstairs.

"You okay?" Luke asked, taking my father's place on the bed.

"Yeah, I guess."

"Wanna tell me about your dream?"

"Not really."

"Rachel, what's going on? You won't really talk to me, and I can't hear your thoughts anymore. I don't know how to help you. You've got to give me something."

"I don't know. I just know that you all are going to die, and I don't know how to live without everyone. Luke, I can't do it. If you guys are gone, I can't do this." I cried.

"Oh, baby, is that what you think? I would never leave you. Rachel, I love you. The whole reason we are doing this is to protect you. I know last night you showed me some of the things that you've seen in your visions. Rachel, we are going to be okay. You just have to have faith in that," Luke said, pulling me into his arms and holding me.

"But see, you don't get it. You will die! I've already seen it. You know I have. A million different times, a million different ways—I've seen it. Luke, you die."

"Did you ever stop to think that maybe what you are seeing isn't a vision and just your worst fears?"

"I know the difference," I said, pulling away from him. However, I wasn't positive I did.

"Okay, okay. Shush, I didn't mean to upset you. I was only trying to give you a different light in which to see things."

"Thanks." I sniffled. "I guess we should eat."

I followed Luke downstairs in a haze. That dream was so vivid. It was so real. I could still see the blood on the walls. It scared me to death. I know death comes to all sooner or later, but to lose everyone I cared about in one blow like that would be too much. I couldn't handle it.

Maybe Luke was right; maybe all of this was just my worst fear preying on my mind. Nonetheless, it was taking its toll on my body as well. All day, I felt weak and tired. I didn't have the energy to do anything. I wasn't hungry. After breakfast, I went straight back upstairs to take a hot bath. I was hoping the warm water would help to relieve the tenseness in my muscles. It was of no use; nothing seemed to help. I tried yoga and meditating. After lunch, I simply gave up hope and crawled back into bed. Hopefully, if I went back to sleep, I would have a good dream filled with the shining sun and picnics and birds and flowers. Then maybe I would feel better in my little piece of heaven surrounded by my family. As soon as I closed my eyes though, I was surrounded by darkness and blood. I opened my eyes again as the tears started to fall. *Why me? Why my family? Why did all of this have to be happening to me?* I would give anything to trade places with someone else. Not that I would ever wish any of this on another person. I lay in bed, watching movies till dinner. *If I have to, I just won't sleep,* I told myself.

———— ◆ ————

A few days past, and nothing changed. If I closed my eyes, I saw blood and the dead bodies of my family. It was late, and I was getting ready to go downstairs for dinner. I had made a point of putting makeup on before leaving my room lately. But tonight I was just too tired. I sighed as I caught a glimpse of myself in the mirror. I had dark purple circles under my eyes due to my lack of sleep. My skin had lost all of its color and luster. I looked pale, and my lack of appetite showed in my sunken cheeks. I shook my head to push away all the depressing thoughts that were trying to engulf me and headed downstairs.

"Rachel, what's wrong? You look like a zombie." Nathan asked at dinner.

"Nothing, Nate. Just tired, I guess," What was I supposed to tell him, that every time I close my eyes I see their dead, lifeless bodies? Somehow I didn't think that was going to help anyone, especially me. I didn't want to talk about it anymore. I just wanted to ignore it and hope it went away.

After dinner and helping clean up, I went back to my room. I wasn't eager to sleep, but I didn't want to be around any of them either. I wanted to push them as far away as possible. If I was going to lose them no matter what, perhaps this way I could save myself some of the pain. Plus if I was around them, it was only a matter of time before they noticed my jumpiness and lack of sleep. This would bring on questions that I didn't want to have to think about the answers to. So I sat in my room playing cards and watching TV. Somewhere around one o'clock in the morning, I guess I lost my battle with sleep because the next thing I knew I was standing in a field surrounded by the dismembered bodies of my family. I woke with a jolt and headed downstairs for breakfast. It was Monday morning.

"Rachel, why aren't you dressed yet?" my dad asked as soon as I sat down.

"Dressed for what?"

"Oh, I don't know. School, maybe?"

"Oh, right. That thing you said I would no longer be attending. Right, how silly of me. I'll go get ready," I said, rolling my eyes and getting up. Upstairs, I threw on the first things I saw, brushed my hair and put it into a ponytail, and brushed my teeth. "Look, I'm ready," I said once I was back downstairs. I grabbed my backpack and headed for the door.

"Rachel, don't you want something to eat?" Clair called from the kitchen.

"Thanks, but I'm not hungry," I responded, heading out to the car. I could hear her sigh as I shut the door.

There wasn't much to do at school. It was the last week of school, and a lot like the first week, I saw it as a huge waste of time. Still I walked from class to class not talking or making eye contact with anyone. I spent lunchtime hiding in the bathroom. I really did look like a zombie. My eyes were dark and sunken from lack of sleep and lack of food; I could tell I was starting to lose weight again, which even I knew was a bad thing. I hadn't gained back all the weight I had lost after Adam's death yet.

On a few occasions during the week, Brooke tried to get me to talk to her, but I didn't have anything to say. Between my dreams and family, I was defeated. By Friday, I had finally figured out what was wrong with me. I had ultimately given up on hope; I had accepted that everyone I loved was going to die despite what I had done trying to protect them.

16

woke up in a cold sweat, screaming. It's been the same every night this week. They're dead, all of them. *I can't allow that to happen. I have to save them no matter what. It's been my mantra for far too long*, I thought, shaking my head. *They are all I have. They can't just leave me here alone.* I noticed the day was stormy and dark. It seemed to reflect how I was feeling. Today was the day.

From the moment I woke up, I had known that it was going to happen today, every fiber of my being knew it. I could feel my stomach sink as my heart starts to pound. I could see the lightning and hear the thunder from my bed. *It's today. I'm out of time. We have come to the end. No more time to prepare. They will be here soon.*

I had to work fast; there are some extra protections Brooke taught me. Begrudgingly, I got out of bed despite my want to snuggle back up in its warmth and hope it was all a nightmare. As I got up, I could hear my family downstairs happily moving around, most likely making breakfast. With any hope, today went the way I planned, and this wouldn't be the last time I'd see everyone, but there was always that fear that I would never see any of them again. I tried my best to take in every sound, every smell; in the chance that they died, I wanted to remember every detail. I grabbed the candles and needle Brooke gave me.

I flash back to two weeks ago in Brooke's room when she taught me what to do before my dad showed up and went all cavemen on me.

"Okay, Rachel, what you're going to do is light the candles in this order: red, yellow, red. That's crucial. Once the candles are lit, start the chant, 'My blood, my protection. My lifeline, my life.' Continue chanting as you prick your finger, adding a blood drop for each person—your mom, dad, Mark, Clair, Luke, Nathan, and Ryan—to the yellow candle flame. Doing this while chanting, you are strengthening the blood tie we have already done. Just in case they have witches as well, doing this will prevent them from being able to break the spell."

Once I had finished the spell, I dressed quickly in jeans and a T-shirt and threw my hair into a tight bun and put on my tennis shoes. I ran downstairs. They were gathered in the kitchen, talking and laughing. I stood there for a while in the hall, just watching until my dad saw me. This was how I wanted to remember them, happy and full of life.

"What's wrong, sweetie?" my dad asked.

"Despite what we've said in the past couple of weeks, I want you all to know that I love you and I always will despite how today goes. They will be in the clearing in an hour. You guys should probably eat and head out if you want to stop them in the clearing and not have them come here."

"Well, I guess that means it's go time." Ryan smiled.

Leave it to him to find some twisted pleasure in all of this. I was smiling at him, thinking how nice it was to have him as a big brother, when it hit. There were candles and blood everywhere. The chanting was so loud. *Ahh my head. Oh my god, what is happening?*

My vision swirled, and I was back in the kitchen with my family, but I was on the floor now with concerned faces staring down at me.

"They have witches. A lot of them. You guys need to be careful. You won't just be fighting them," I warned.

"Rachel, your nose and ears are bleeding," my mom told me in a panic.

"It's okay, Mom. I'm all right, I promise. It just does that sometimes." I tried my best to reassure her, granted this vision felt like they were attempting to fry my brain. *If Jason has witches, I should've known. I should've seen it. Why now? Something's not right*, I thought, shaking my head. I didn't know if I should say something or keep it to myself.

Slowly I got up and wiped the blood away as we all silently went to sit down for breakfast. I had been hoping for a nice and happy family meal, one that I would want to remember, but with the heaviness of what was about to come and my most recent vision, I had a feeling that wasn't going to happen. I sighed as I sat down. It seemed that everyone was happy to eat in silence today, and I didn't have anything to say to break it. Once breakfast was over, the guys helped carry all the dishes to the kitchen, and then it was time for good-byes. Good-byes are terrifying, especially when you know there is a real chance you will never see each other again. I hugged my dad, Mark, Nathan, Ryan, and finally Luke. I held on to him for dear life as the tears streamed down my face.

"I love you," I whispered into his chest.

"I love you too, sweetheart. Don't worry, we will be back in a few hours. You'll see." And with that he let me go, and they were gone.

I hung out with my mom and Clair downstairs for as long as I could. My anxiety was killing me. I hated not knowing what was going on. Slowly I made my way back up to my room. I lit my candles and cleared my mind of everything. Thanks to Brooke and lots of practice, I could now force the vision or attach to a person's mind. When I did this, I could see and hear what they did. The one downside to this was I also got hurt in the same ways they did.

Today, I would be attaching to Jason, but first I focused on Luke. I wanted to know that everyone was still okay. I wanted to know what was happening. I needed to know what was happening. Concentrating as hard as I could with my eyes shut, I could see the clearing. They were fighting near the top in a clearing. Major downside to this was if they weren't careful, they could easily fall off the side. There were bodies and people everywhere. It was so hard to keep track of who was winning and who was losing. To be honest, it was hard to keep track of who is who. It was so dark due to the storm that if you didn't know it you couldn't even tell it was daytime. They were being pelted by rain, and I was sure it didn't help at all. I was also sure Nathan was the reason the storm was so strong in the first place.

I could see my dad; he was covered in blood, but from what I could tell, most of it wasn't his. He was using one of the crossbows and taking out vampire after vampire. I scanned again, finding Mark. He was teleporting in and out of groups of werewolves, shooting them with silver bullets. Nathan wasn't far away using his power to send lightning bolts into a group of shape-shifters. I searched and searched, but I couldn't seem to find Ryan. I was sure he was there somewhere, but before I could find him, I felt something sharp and painful enter my back. I could feel it as it pierced my heart, and I snapped back to my room. Reaching around to touch my back, I felt the telltale sign of blood. I knew that I had been stabbed, or I guess Luke must have been stabbed.

Taking a deep breath, I realized it most likely had killed him, which was what forced me out of his head. The only thing I could do was pray that the linking spell Brooke did works because I couldn't live with the thought of him not coming home. I didn't have time to think about it now. Shaking my head, I tried to clear it of those thoughts.

I grabbed another shirt and changed real quick. Right now, I needed to find out where Jason was and how much time I have. I knew that the clearing was just a decoy, but it didn't matter what we did. In every vision, I tried to force a different outcome, but it didn't seem to matter—everyone died, and they got me. The way that it was happening today was the one with the best result. At least when I tried it this way, some of them lived. I sat there watching and waiting until Jason gave the order for Kaylee, Brad, and himself to break off from the group and come here. Quickly, I snapped out of the vision and ran downstairs to find my mom and Clair.

"They are on their way. There's three of them. We need to be ready to fight," I told them and returned to my room. My mom and Clair would never see any of the fight, but they didn't know that. By telling them, at least they would be distracted for a little while.

They didn't want me to be a part of this fight, so I wouldn't. I knew that they weren't going to hurt my mom or Clair, thanks to the protection spell Brooke put on the house, and as everyone had been saying all along, they only wanted me. Back in my room, I blew out my candles and headed for the window. I knew the guys would be pissed if they knew what I had planned, but I saw it as the only way. Once they had me, the battle would be over, and thanks to my visions, I knew exactly where they were going to take me this time. I had left very detailed directions on where, when, and how to find me. Hopefully they would listen to me at least this once. Using my powers, I forced the window open from where my dad had nailed it shut. I sent up a quick prayer as I made my way into the woods to wait. They would be here any minute now. As I waited, my mind wandered to the clearing in the forest where my family was fighting to save my life, risking theirs for mine.

"Well, well, I see you were smart enough to come to me, my dear," Jason spoke once he was close enough for me to hear him.

"Yes, well, you and I both know you were going to get to me either way, so here I am. But if you want me, you are going to have to do something for me first."

"And what makes you think that I will do anything for you?"

"Because I know you, Even as a vampire, you are still a gentleman deep down. Aren't you? You'll keep your word even if you hate it."

"Well, Rachel. I must admit you do seem to have me figured out now, don't you. But what makes you think I would do something for you? From where I stand, you hold no cards to play."

"Call off the battle, let my family go, and leave them alone. If you want me, these are my conditions."

"Again, silly child, why would I make that deal with you when I can simply take you and kill your family?"

"Because if you don't, I'll kill myself, making all of this pointless," I said, pulling a blade from behind my back. It was Luke's, and just having it in my hand, I felt some of his strength giving me the courage to do this.

"Very well." With that, he closed his eyes and seemed to concentrate really hard. "It is done. Shall we?" he asked, holding out his hand to me.

"How am I supposed to know that you actually called them off? All you did was close your eyes."

"As a vampire, we can communicate with other vampires using only our mind. Seeing as you clearly don't trust me, go ahead and check. I know you can enter people's minds. I've felt you in mine several times. Go ahead, check on your family. I'll wait, but do be quick. I'm getting bored."

I quickly shut my eyes and concentrated on my dad as hard as I could. I saw Mark helping Luke off the ground. They all stared in confusion as the werewolves, shape-shifters, and vampires retreated.

I nodded my head as I made my way over to him. I could still run, but he and I both knew I wouldn't. I knew what I was doing was potential suicide, but if it saved my family, I didn't care. Jason swiftly put me on his back and started to run rapidly through the woods. Before I knew it, we were at his lair, and he was throwing me into a cage.

"Are you okay?" a guy asked, grabbing my arm and helping me up.

"Yeah, I'm fine, thanks," I said, standing up and turning to face the guy. "Wait, that's not possible. What are you doing here?"

"I'm sorry. Do I know you?"

"Ryan! What are you doing here? Why aren't you with everyone else?"

"How do you know me? Have we met? Do you know my parents and brothers? Are they okay?"

"Ryan, you aren't making any sense. Of course I know you. I've been dating your brother for the past year, and you and I have become like brother and sister. What have they done to you?"

"You know Luke and Nathan? Look, I don't know who you are, but I've been here in this cage for two years…I think. I have no idea who you met, but it wasn't me."

"That's not possible. Shit. No, they couldn't have… Really… Wow… Well, this changes everything."

"Um, sorry, but you aren't making a lot of sense anymore. Not that you were making a ton of sense before."

"I'm Rachel Clissdale," I introduced myself, holding out my hand to shake his.

"You're Peter's daughter?"

"Yes."

"Then we failed. They got you."

"Well... Kinda. I came here of my own free will. I saw that no matter what the guys did, they were going to die. Granted that makes more sense now, knowing that the person I thought to be you must be a shape-shifter and on their side. Anyhow, I gave myself up, on the condition that Jason calls off his attack on our families, and then I left them detailed instructions on where to find me. But with you not being you, that kind of changes everything."

"What were you thinking giving yourself up? We knew going into this that there was a very real chance that we would all die. We were willing to make that sacrifice in order to save you."

"Well, all of you may have been ready to make that sacrifice, but I wasn't."

"You really don't get it, do you? What are two families in the grand scheme of things? Rachel, we are seven people, but if they have you, millions even billions could die."

Okay, I hadn't thought of it like that, and I am feeling extremely selfish right now, but I'm still not sure how much I care. They were my family, and I was not willing to lose them. They should be here soon. I really hoped this wasn't a huge mistake. I was counting on what my grandfather said being right. Hopefully, when they were fighting for the love they have for me and not the fear they had of losing me, we would win, but with the new shape-shifter information, anything could happen. Fleetingly, an old vision flashed in my head—it was of a guy running on a trail at dusk. He didn't stand a chance; he was being chased by what appeared to be a wolf. Granted, I doubted that's what it really was. The wolf gained on him quickly, and I watched frozen to the spot as the guy turned and tried to wrestle the ginormous dog. I watched as the guy sent rocks flying and caused the earth to open up, but in the end, it didn't matter. The wolf got what it came for: him. I remembered this vision now that I saw it again. At that time, I thought it was just another vision like all the others, but now I realized the guy in the vision was Ryan. Guilt and fear crept into my soul. If I knew Ryan, was it possible that everyone in my visions was in some way connected to me? That was something I would dwell on more after today was over.

"Crap. That's why you looked so familiar. God, I'm an idiot. Why didn't I put it together sooner?"

"I'm sorry, you lost me again."

"When I met you for the first time, or well what I thought was you, I thought you looked familiar. Two years ago, when you were taken, I saw it. I mean, I didn't know it was you until now, but I'm so sorry. I should've put it together."

"It's not your fault."

"But don't you see? It is. It's all my fault. I should've stopped all of it. With my visions, I should've been able to stop all of this. It should never have gotten this far."

"You didn't even know what you were. How were you going to stop any of this?"

"I don't know, but do you know what it's like knowing all of these horrible things are going to happen and not being able to do anything about it? Do you know what it's like watching people tortured to death all because of you?" I asked, finally collapsing back to the floor in tears. I couldn't take it. It was all my fault. Everyone was going to die, and it was because of me.

Ryan got down on the floor with me and held me while I cried. I felt so stupid. I had been trying to be strong, to save my family. Now everything was just catching up with me. My emotions were all over the place. I felt happy knowing all of this would soon be over despite the outcome. I felt sad knowing so many people had already died, and I couldn't save them. I felt angry knowing that I had been tricked. I felt stupid not being able to see it before. It was a setup the whole time. Just more proof that I wasn't Madeline, like I needed any more evidence of that.

The longer I sat there crying, the angrier I got. As my anger built, so did my powers. I still hadn't figured out how to totally control my telekinesis, and soon the bars holding us in this cage started to shake. I tried to center myself and project my rage. I wanted out of this damn cage, and with that thought, the bars that were holding us in exploded outward. We were free. Now what was I going to do? Thankfully, I didn't have to try to figure it out. Ryan and I had no sooner made it out of our cage before there was a blinding light. I knew from watching the boys train that it was one of dad and

Mark's UV grenades, but damn those things hurt my eyes. All I could see were spots. I had no idea who it was that was grabbing my arm and helping me up, but I was grateful for the help.

"Ryan's a shape-shifter. Kill him," I quietly pleaded with the person.

"What?" I finally heard Luke's voice.

"The Ryan you came here with isn't the real Ryan. Do something," I said again.

I watched as Nathan grabbed the person that had been an older brother to him for the past two years and slit his throat as if it was nothing. Finally, they were trusting me, listening to me, and of course it was resulting in someone's death. Suddenly having them listen to me didn't seem like such a victory. Maybe they were right all along; I shouldn't be here. Suddenly I was not sure I could handle killing someone. I didn't have time to contemplate my willingness to kill because, in my next breath, Luke was charging. Someone had come in behind us and attacked. I looked around, hoping someone was going to do something, but all my family was locked in a battle with someone else. I had to stop this. I wasn't going to let anyone in my family die.

"Stop it!" I screamed, causing the entire place to shake. It worked for only a moment, but it was enough of a distraction for my family to get the upper hand. I backed into a corner watching as my family fought. Everyone seemed to be holding their own for now, but I doubted it would last for long. I stood there for a few moments watching in horrified fascination. Ryan was using his powers to throw rocks and boulders at the monsters. Mark was teleporting here and there, killing anything he could get his hands on. Luke was a fiery blaze of sexiness as I watched him kill several vampires with his fire. However when I found my dad, I was terrified when two vampires held him as he struggled to get away. They were outnumbered two to one, and I knew there had to be more because I didn't see Jason, Kaylee, or Brad.

"Rachel, run!" my dad yelled.

"No, Daddy, I'm not leaving you."

"Good, then you will be mine," Jason said, finally joining the fight and grabbing me. "All right that's enough! If you don't want her to die, you will all come quietly," he said in a commanding tone.

No. This can't be happening. It wasn't supposed to happen like this. We were supposed to win. They weren't supposed to get my family and me. Oh my god, what would Clair and my mom think of me if I was the reason they lost all their boys? What was I going to do? I couldn't let this happen. Jason and all of his minions dragged us into a room. I knew this place from my first vision. It was a cavern inside the cave that Jason called home. It was dark and lit by candles; in front of the cavern, there was a large chair that clearly was used for some type of torture in the medieval days. There were straps connected to it in order to restrain someone's wrist and ankles. I knew as soon as we entered the room where Jason was taking me. I was going into that damn chair again. I tried to fight Jason as he dragged me closer to the chair.

"Stop fighting and be a good little girl, will you?" Jason snarled.

"No, let me and my family go, or I will kill you." I spat back at him.

"You're going to kill me?" He laughed. "From where I stand, that doesn't seem very likely," he said, throwing me into the chair while two others who had been standing near it strapped me in. They had my family in front of me now on their knees. "Now, Rachel, I really am a kind person, so I will let you choose, who dies first?"

"Go to hell," I whispered through my tears.

"I'm sorry, what was that?"

"Go...to...hell!"

"No, thank you. I rather like it here." Jason laughed. "Now choose, or I'll choose for you," he said, walking up behind Luke.

"No!" I cried.

"No? Not Luke. Okay then, choose."

"I can't, please."

"Rachel, they are going to die. I'm just giving you the courtesy of choosing who dies first."

I couldn't look at my family; I couldn't stand the sight of what I was sure would be disappointment in their eyes. "Please, they're my family...please," I begged.

"Why should I let your family live? You think you know pain, child. You know nothing of pain. I was changed into this five hundred years ago. I watched as everyone I loved died knowing that the only way to save them was to curse them with this life, and I couldn't do that. I watched my parents, wife, children, and grandchildren die slowly of old age, never knowing how much I loved them or how much they meant to me. Now choose!"

"Jason, they knew you loved them. They knew how much you cared about them. You don't have to do this," I pleaded.

"Trying to act caring and understanding won't save you," he said, grabbing my dad and biting into his neck.

"No! Daddy!" I screamed, but it did no good. I watched in terror and rage as Jason drained my dad of every last drop of blood. My anger was so intense I could feel my skin burning with my rage.

"I love you, sweetheart," my father whispered on his last breath.

17

Anger and rage flooded my body. I could feel nothing else. Anger and pain blinded me, causing Jason and his gang to rise to the ceiling.

Luke rushed to undo my restraints. "Are you okay?"

"No," I snarled. "Get everyone out of here. Take my dad's body and go!" I shoved Luke off me, causing him to go flying into the wall.

"Rachel, sweetie, we can't leave you," Mark tried to convey to me. "Come home with us. We will take care of the trash later."

"I can't. I'm sorry, Mark, but I can't. Now go. Tell my mom I'm so sorry, I never meant for any of this to happen." With one motion of my hand, I lifted all five of them and moved them out of the cavern. And using a rock, I locked myself in the cavern with Jason and his followers. I was going to finish this even if it killed me. I brought Jason back down to the ground non to gently using my powers to hold him in place.

"Where is Madeline?" I asked. When he didn't answer, I screamed, "Where is she!" It caused the walls around us to shake again.

"Okay, Rachel, you win. Just let me go," Jason said. "You can have everyone else, just let me go."

"Let you go? Let you go? You aren't going anywhere but to hell. You just killed my father, you coward. Do you think begging is going to do you any good? I don't think so, but I can return the favor by sending you where you belong, the fiery pits of hell," I snapped in mild hysterics.

"I'll tell you where she is if you let me go."

"You'll tell me where she is either way," I said, grabbing one of the bags the boys had left behind. Bending down, I opened it. Inside there was a silver pellet grenade. I grabbed it, pulled the pin, and threw it into the air above me, where all of Jason's helpers were still waiting to die. It went off, killing three werewolves and injuring countless others. I felt some of the shards enter the flesh on my arms. The physical pain was a welcomed comfort; it was nice to know that I could still feel something, even if it was pain. Reaching back into the bag, I pulled out a wooden stake.

"Where is Madeline?" I asked for the final time, slowly pushing the stake into Jason's chest. With his silence, I lost all self-control and drove the stake directly into Jason's unbeating heart. I would have to find Madeline another way. Looking into the bag, I saw that there were two silver grenades and three wooden ones left. I grabbed them, moved the rock from my exit, pulled all the pins, threw them in, and ran like hell. I was done playing, and I wanted to be home. I wanted my dad. Outside the cave's entrance, I ran into Luke, Nathan, Ryan, Mark, and my father's lifeless body.

"Are you okay?" Ryan asked.

I looked to Ryan in answer to his question. Was I all right? I was alive, but by no meaning of the word was I okay. My father lay beside Mark's feet, lifeless and drained of blood. He was dead. My dad was dead, and it was my fault. Everything that happened was because of me. Collapsing on my father's body, I broke down.

"Oh my god, Daddy, I'm so sorry. I'm so so so sorry. I never wanted any of this to happen. I just wanted to protect all of you. I went to Brooke for help, and she cast spells and—" I stopped suddenly. *The spell. He can't be dead.*

"Rachel, are you okay?" Mark asked, kneeling down beside me.

"He's not dead! He's not dead!"

"Yes, sweetie, he is. You saw Jason kill him right in front of you. Sweetie, he is dead," Mark tried to explain gently.

"No, but don't you see? The spell... He can't be dead."

"Luke, what is she talking about?" Mark asked, clearly not being able to make sense of what I was saying.

"I don't know, Dad. She found a way to block her mind from—"

"Daddy!" I screamed, cutting Luke off, as my dad took an enormous gulp of air and sat up.

"What the hell happened?" my dad asked, holding onto me. Everyone else was looking at him like they had seen a ghost.

"Brooke's spell, Daddy, it worked! It saved you."

"What spell, Rachel?" my dad asked.

"The one that kinda temporarily killed me. It was a linking spell."

"And what does a linking spell do exactly?" Luke asked, looking furious.

"Well...it uh...links things," I said, trying to avoid answering his question.

"Rachel!" everyone said in unison.

"Okay, look, can I at least explain at home?" I asked hopefully. I was ready to get away from this place, and I needed the time to figure out the best way to tell them what I had done. Despite the fact that it saved my dad and Luke, I had a feeling that no one was going to be especially happy about it.

"Actually, I think that's a good idea. I for one want to get as far away from this place as possible," Ryan said.

"You're right, let's go," Mark said, helping my father up.

Everyone nodded. I climbed onto Luke's back, and everyone started running home. I was so thankful everyone was safe and alive, but somehow I had this sinking feeling that it wasn't over yet. Once we were home, mom and Clair met us outside.

"Oh, thank God!" they said, grabbing us and hugging us until we couldn't breath.

"Ryan, what happened to you?" Clair asked finally getting a better look at her oldest son. He was dirty and at least thirty pounds lighter than he had been when he left the house that morning. He had a healthy beard growing, but his eyes were kinder.

"Oh, you know, I've been locked in a cave for two years and had some shape-shifter take over living my life. No big deal."

"How is that even possible?" Clair asked, looking to her husband.

"I don't know, Mom, but to be honest, I'm just happy to be home."

"Well, let's get all of you back inside and cleaned up. Who wants some tea?" my mom said, directing us all inside.

"Sounds great," I told her, making my way to the kitchen. I had extremely high hopes everyone had forgotten about what I had said and done.

"Not so fast, Rachel. As I recall, you owe us all an explanation," my dad said. "Not that I'm complaining," he added as an afterthought.

"Right. Okay, so I went to Brooke, knowing that she was a witch—I've actually known that for a while. When none of you listened to me, I went to her looking for help. I needed to find a way to keep you all safe. I couldn't live with the thought that you all could die trying to protect me. So after a lot of looking at different ideas, we finally came up with the idea to cast three spells. One to lock my mind so Luke couldn't tip you off to what we were doing, a protection spell on the houses so that no evil could enter, which does beg the question of how the shape-shifter of Ryan was able to come in in the first place," I said, getting distracted.

"Rachel!" all the guys shouted.

"Oh, right... Right. And the third was a linking spell. So Brooke first linked her and me so she could draw off of me for the strength she would need to do the spells. At first, I was fine, but as she did more, it slowly took more out of me. Finally, she did the linking spell, and apparently, it killed me for fifteen minutes or so. See, no big deal. I'm still alive. So who wants tea?"

"No, Rachel. Sit back down. What does a linking spell do?" Mark asked in a rather scary tone that, thankfully, I had never heard before.

"Well, it links all of your lifelines to mine. Basically, as long as I'm alive, so are all of you. Unless all of you died at the same time, which would then kill me, which I thought was perfect. This way, they didn't get me or my powers. See, the perfect plan, and you're all still alive. So no harm, no foul, right?"

"What the hell were you thinking?" Clair screamed, causing everyone in the room to look up in shock. I didn't think I had ever heard Clair even half yell, much less the tone she just used.

"I was...ugh...I was thinking it was a good plan?" I asked, terrified.

"Oh, you thought it was a good plan. She thought it was a good plan," she said, turning toward my mom. "And what the hell makes you think it was a good plan?"

"Um...everyone's still alive, so I would take that as a good plan, considering if it weren't for the spell, Dad and Luke would both be dead," I said, feeling angry that no one was happy that I had helped save their lives.

"What do you mean Luke and your dad?" She turned to her son.

It was Luke's turn to look sheepish. "Mom, you knew the risk we were all taking. It's no big deal," he said, trying to calm her down.

"Well, I am so happy no one here thinks dying is a big damn deal."

"That's not what I said, Mom, and Rachel, how did you know I had died?" he asked, turning back to me.

"With enough concentration, I can enter your mind and see things as you see them, or well anyone's mind technically," I said, turning my back to them. I lifted the back of my shirt to show them the spot where Luke and I both had scars. "What I didn't know is that whatever happens to the person whose mind I'm in happens to me as well, at least to some degree."

Luke lightly traced the mark on my back.

"How do you unlink us?" my mom asked through tears.

"I don't know. I didn't think to ask that. To be honest, I didn't think any of us would live long enough for that to matter," I told her honestly.

"What happened to Jason?" my dad asked.

"He's dead. I killed him."

"How?" Nathan asked.

"I put a stake through his heart."

"And Madeline?" Mark asked.

"I don't know. I lost my temper and killed him before he told me," I said, shaking my head. "I didn't mean to. My anger just got the best of me."

"What happened to all the others?" my dad asked, looking to Mark and Luke.

"I killed them, I think. I didn't wait around to find out," I said, causing my dad's head to whip around to me so fast I thought he was going to break his neck.

"You killed them? Where in the hell were all of you?" he asked, staring down at Mark. "I die, and you let my little girl go off and kill all these things while the guys that have been training their whole lives to do it...what, run and hide? What if something would've happened to her?"

"Look, Peter, I don't like it any more than you do, but it's not like she really gave us any choice."

"What do you mean she didn't give you any choice? For God's sake, Mark, she is a seventeen-year-old girl," my dad yelled.

"Daddy…" I said forcing my powers to work and raising them off the ground. One good outcome of today was I think I finally had figured out how to make them work when I wanted. "I forced them out of the cave and blocked it with a boulder," I told him and sat them all back down on the floor. "I'm sorry, Daddy, but I thought that I had lost you. Jason killed you right in front of me. What was I supposed to do?"

"Oh, baby, it's okay," he said, grabbing me and hugging me. "At least you are all right."

"Okay, well, now that all of that's out of the way, why don't you guys go take a shower and then come back down and we'll get those wounds taken care of," my mom said, apparently still fighting back tears.

Upstairs in my room, I took off my blood-stained and torn clothes and got into the shower. I couldn't believe I had killed someone even if they were already dead. I sank to the floor in tears. I just sat there with the water running mixing with all my fears, happiness, and self-loathing. I had killed someone. I would have to live with that knowledge for the rest of my life. I wasn't sure if I could handle that, but I suppose it was better than losing everyone I loved. *You did what you had to*, I told myself and stood up, quickly finishing my shower. I couldn't stand being by myself for one more moment.

By the time I was dressed and made it back downstairs, my wounds were already starting to heal. I sat and watched as my mom and Clair bandaged everyone else up. I was just happy to have my family whole for now. Everything else could wait.

CPSIA information can be obtained
at www.ICGtesting.com
Printed in the USA
LVOW01s1219040716
494819LV00028B/86/P

9 781681 870847